DEATH IN AN ENGLISH COTTAGE

DEATH IN AN ENGLISH COTTAGE

BOOK TWO IN THE MURDER ON LOCATION SERIES

SARA ROSETT

McGuffin Ink

DEATH IN AN ENGLISH COTTAGE
Book Two in the *Murder on Location* series
An English Village Murder Mystery
Published by McGuffin Ink

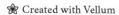 Created with Vellum

"Seldom, very seldom, does complete truth belong to any human disclosure; seldom can it happen that something is not a little disguised or a little mistaken."
—Jane Austen, *Emma*

CHAPTER 1

*H*OW COULD I HAVE FORGOTTEN about the rain? I wiped my hand across the interior of the taxi's window to remove a layer of condensation. It didn't help me to see much better. Raindrops coursed down the exterior of the window, blurring the landscape into an abstract in shades of green.

It was funny—or perhaps ironic—that I'd so thoroughly eliminated the rain from my memories. It wasn't as if it hadn't rained during my visit to England a month earlier. It had rained often— quite often, actually. But as I packed up my belongings and sorted some of my things into suitcases and others into storage in parched and sunny Southern California, my memories of England were of clear blue skies dotted with puffy clouds over rolling green hills and a quaint English village glowing golden in the sunshine.

I shifted uncomfortably in the seat and tried to curb the uneasiness that had crept over me. What had seemed an innovative and exciting career move in the shimmering heat of Los Angeles now seemed impulsive and rather foolish.

My phone rang, and I saw it was Marci, the office manager

from my old location scouting firm. "How is jolly old England?" Marci asked after I answered.

"Rainy. Dreary."

"Ah, that would be nice. We haven't had rain here, not even a sprinkle, in…I don't know…I can't remember the last time it rained. How are you holding up, kid?"

"I have that terrible, what-have-I-done, sick feeling in the pit of my stomach," I admitted.

"Jetlag," she pronounced. "Don't do anything rash."

"What, other than moving to a foreign country on the spur-of-the-minute for a short-term job?"

Marci's rich laugh filled the line. The driver glanced back at me before refocusing on the road. "Exactly," she said, then her tone turned serious. "Don't come back too soon."

"And I thought you were going to miss me."

"Oh, I do. You should see the expense reports these people turn in. I'm only saying that you seemed to want something…different."

"I did. I wanted a change."

"You sound so regretful."

"Just second-guessing myself. You're right. It's got to be the jetlag. I'll call you in a few days."

"Probably spouting about how wonderful it is and how you love hot tea or something. You take care, kid."

"Thanks, Marci."

I straightened my shoulders. It was perfectly natural to feel a little off-balance during a transition. But that's what I wanted, a change. Something new.

I had fallen into a location scout job a few years ago. I was very good at focusing on the task at hand. So much so, that I had spent the last few years working intently to keep my head above water financially, but last month I'd finally switched my vision from my usual up-close day-to-day focus to the long-term horizon. I hadn't liked what I'd seen. My job consumed me. It was that sort of work. Fifteen-hour days and a pace that required intensity and focus. When the offer came through Alex to work in England, it had seemed to be a wonderful change. I loved the idea of being in England for a month straight, and although I knew the pace would be just as hectic as in Southern California, there was another reason I'd accepted the job.

Alex Norcutt. There was something between us. I wasn't quite sure what it was. There was a friendship, yes, certainly that. But maybe something more. I'd decided I wanted to explore those possibilities, and the job offer gave me the perfect opportunity to do that.

The taxi swung into a turn and crossed a bridge. I recognized the wide, fast-moving river. We were in Nether Woodsmoor, the golden stone cottages and shops flicking by the window. Gloomy clouds hung low, casting a gray tinge on the butter colored stones. Striped awnings pulsed and hanging baskets, bright with flowers, spun in the stiff breeze. A few people hurried across the street, their umbrellas pushing into the wind. The chairs and tables of the two sidewalk cafes on the village's high street were stacked under the eaves. Swinging signs for the White Duck pub, the bike shop, and the tea shop flicked back and forth at a manic pace.

I checked the text again on my phone as we cruised by the sturdy centuries-old church with its pointed spire that seemed to almost touch the low clouds. Alex had said to come to the inn, that they were meeting there, but the whole village looked as if it had battened down the hatches against the storm.

I flicked through the texts Alex and I had exchanged for the last few weeks. A month ago when I'd accepted the job, we had talked on the phone frequently. There were a lot of details to work out, but as pre-production on *Jane Austen: Secrets Revealed* ramped up, his phone calls tapered off and the number of texts increased.

I went to the last texts we'd exchanged. I'd planned to rent a car as I had the last time I was in England, but he'd said to take a cab. We'd had a bit of an argument—as much of an argument as you can by text—with me insisting that I'd need a car and Alex contending that the production had several cars I could use once I got to Nether Woodsmoor. I didn't like the idea of being without a car. I was a California girl, after all. Public transportation was all well and good, but I wanted options and freedom; however, in the end, I'd capitulated when Alex had said he didn't know if the production could cover a long-term rental, but he would check. Not wanting to get off on the wrong foot with the producer, I'd told him to forget the whole thing.

I had taken the taxi and watched the meter climb, thinking that Kevin, my former boss, would lose it if I turned in a receipt for a taxi ride over an hour long. I shook my head and squashed down the sadness I felt. I wasn't working for Kevin. I pushed those thoughts away. This was a new project, a new beginning. A bolt of lightning flickered in the distance and thunder rumbled.

I found Alex's most recent text, a reply to the text I'd sent him to tell him I'd landed in Manchester. He'd texted back, *At a Secrets Revealed lunch meeting. We are at the inn. Have the taxi drop you there. See you soon.*

I wrinkled my nose over the documentary title that I had signed on with. It sounded sensational and overly dramatic. What secrets were there to be revealed about Jane Austen? Hadn't every possible nuance of her writings and every crumb of info about her life been examined by scholars and fans alike? Of course the documentary was for television. Sensationalism sells, not as much as sex, but hey, you work with what you've got, and there was precious little sex in a documentary about Jane Austen, so I guess that left sensationalism.

I had met Alex when the Los Angeles-based location scouting company I worked for was tapped to find locations for a new feature film version of *Pride and Prejudice*. When the remake fell through, the producer of the Jane Austen documentary had contacted Alex, asking him to come to work for her, rightly assuming that much of the work he'd done scouting locations for the movie could be used for the three-episode documentary. It was a large, fast-moving project, and Alex had suggested I come on board to help with the location scouting and the Jane Austen details. I was a bit of an Anglophile—at least that's the way I preferred to think of it. My mom would say less kindly that I was a Jane Austen nut and spent far too much time immersed in books.

I scanned Alex's text again. Short and to the point. If I'd been sending it, I would have included a smiley face at the end, but then again, maybe emoticons were more of a girl thing. The tone of his texts had become more perfunctory over the last week or so, and I hoped he wasn't regretting the job offer he'd secured for me. I put my phone away. Too much analysis.

I looped my tote bag over my shoulder and tucked a few strands of hair that had come loose from my ponytail behind my ears—that was the extent of my damage control. There's not much a girl can do to mask a ten-hour trans-Atlantic journey.

We were out of the village proper, and I could see the white stucco and wood beamed two-story inn set back from the road with its diamond-paned windows glowing brightly in the murky atmosphere.

Crouched under my umbrella, I paid the cab driver and carefully tucked the receipt away in my Moleskine journal, then hurried through the rain to the inn, the wheels of my suitcase bumping over the paved courtyard as the rain sluiced down the gutters. Another distant rumble of thunder sounded as I opened the inn's door. A wash of sound drowned out the thunder—boisterous laughter, the constant murmur of low conversation, and the clink of cutlery.

While outside was deserted and rain-drenched, inside was packed. I paused to park my suitcase beside the empty check-in desk as I scanned the crowded restaurant that occupied the main floor of the inn. Every table under the beamed ceiling was full. Even the chairs around the fireplace were occupied with people clutching pints of beer, their waterproof gear, backpacks, and bike helmets draped over the chintz-covered wingback chairs and scattered around them on the hardwood floor.

"Kate!" I recognized Alex's distinctly unaccented voice, which stood out from the crisp British accents around me. He was American, but had grown up moving around the United States and foreign countries as his dad shifted from one diplomatic job to another. I spotted him moving through the crowded tables at his relaxed lope.

He looked just as he had the last time I'd seen him: slightly mussed light brown hair, chocolate-colored eyes, and a wide, easy smile. He extended an arm. I'm not the hugging type. I usually like a good bit of personal space around me, but I couldn't exactly stick out my hand for him to shake at this point —at least that's what I told myself as I leaned in—and we embraced in a side hug, which pressed my nose into the rough weave of his sweater. He smelled of laundry detergent, coffee, and a hint of some sort of lime shaving cream or cologne.

We pulled apart, and he gave me one of his long, assessing stares. "Kate. Good to see you."

Alex was one of the few people I knew who really focused on the person he was talking to, giving each person his undivided attention. I'd forgotten how intense his gaze felt. "I'm so glad you're here."

The noise and bustle of the room seemed to fade a bit as I smiled back at him. "Me too."

"Good flight?"

"Not bad. My seatmate didn't drool on me or insist on talking for ten hours straight. I even got a little sleep."

"So you feel up to meeting everyone?" He tilted his head toward the table where he'd been seated, and the volume of the ambient noise went back up, engulfing me as I transferred my gaze to the group of people seated at a long table littered with papers, coffee mugs, tea cups, crumb-smeared plates, and cell phones.

"Yes, of course."

"Great. Here, let me." Alex lifted my tote bag off my shoulder and led the way to the table where he hooked it on the back of what had been his chair. "Everyone, this is Kate Sharp." Alex pulled out the chair for me and smoothly confiscated what seemed to be the only empty chair in the whole place from a nearby table, pulling it up beside me, and taking a seat.

A man at the far end of the table raised his mug at me. "Ah, the Hollywood location scout come to rescue us." He had a rough around the edges look about him, like he could have been turned out in pressed clothes and with combed hair and less stubble if he cared, but he didn't. I put his age at mid to late thirties, but it was hard to tell because his black hair hung low and scruffy over his pronounced brow. The collar of his shirt was crumpled up on one side, smashed into the worn lapel of a mustard colored blazer. His light brown eyes twinkled. "Nice to meet the amazing Kate. I'm Felix Carrick."

"Felix is our cinematographer," Alex said.

"Hi, Felix. Nice to meet you, but I think you've got a mistaken impression about me. I'm not amazing."

"You are, according to Alex. He says you're a walking, talking Jane Austen encyclopedia."

I shot a glance at Alex, who shook his head. "Felix's specialty is exaggeration."

"I do know a little about Jane Austen, but I'm certainly not an expert." I'd done grad work in English Lit and planned to write my dissertation about Jane Austen, but that had been a long time ago. Another lifetime, it seemed. "I do love her books."

"Doesn't everyone?" Felix said.

"Don't be sarcastic, Felix," said a young woman with several eyebrow rings and short blond hair, except for her bangs, which were bright fuchsia. She wore a poncho made of rough, natural-looking fibers over a pink long-sleeved T-shirt.

"Ah, sarcasm…the province of the young, or so they think," Felix said.

The poncho flared as the woman extended her hand to me. "I'm Melissa Millbank. Continuity."

I shook her hand and said hello while Felix watched us from his sprawled position. Melissa turned back to Felix. "Just because you don't like Austen doesn't mean you have to diss her."

"Yes, yes, I know. It's the universal love of dear Jane that will make our project a success. I know the drill. I'll spout the correct propaganda when I'm interviewed for the featurette." He heaved a mock theatrical sigh. "And I thought escaping the corporate world would mean I didn't have to toe the party line. I should have known better."

"So you're new to film production?" I asked to be polite.

"Been doing it for years, only up until three years ago it was for corporations. But let's get back to you, Kate." His face turned serious. "The question is what camp are you?"

"Camp?"

He leaned forward. "Yes, what kind of Janite are you? Are you a 'gentle Jane' adherent? Do you think she was a quiet spinster writing novels about true love? Or, are you in the feminist camp," he asked with a quick glance at the other woman at the table, whose head was bent over a sheet of paper beside a young lanky guy. The two were involved in an intense discussion. "Was Jane years ahead of her time, writing in code, as it were, subverting the status quo, with feminist subtexts?"

"I think she was an excellent writer."

"Ah, you're no fun."

"She's got your number, doesn't she, Felix?" Melissa turned to me. "Felix is our resident troublemaker. Don't take the bait, and you'll drive him crazy. But it seems you've already figured that out. It's something I have a hard time remembering."

The conversation between the woman who was seated beside Melissa and the long-limbed young man ended. Gathering his papers, he stood, stuck a pencil behind his ear and grinned at me. "Paul Alexander. First A.D." I had a quick impression of his height —he had to be over six-five, but he wasn't burly. He was all boney shoulders and arms, and looked like he hadn't had a square meal in weeks. I shook his hand, and he gulped down the last of his coffee from his standing position before he hurried away through the tables.

The woman who'd been talking to him looked at me, seeming to notice me for the first time. Alex said, "Kate, this is Elise DuPont, our producer." I figured she was in her fifties. Lines radiated from the corners of her eyes, around her lips, and traced along her forehead, but unlike so many women I had worked with in L.A., who were airbrushed, coiffed, and moisturized to the hilt, she hadn't taken any pains to hide her age. It seemed she'd embraced it—or perhaps ignored it. Her faded dark blond hair, which was twisted up into a loose knot on the top of her head and skewered with a pencil, was streaked with gray. She wore a puffy black vest over a black shirt with frayed cuffs and didn't have on any makeup or jewelry. She bent her head over a stack of folders.

"Nice to meet you. I'm really looking forward to this project." I extended my hand, but she didn't take it.

"Good. You're finally here."

I glanced at Alex, uncertainly. "I came directly from the airport."

"Yes, well, it would have been better if you'd been here last week."

Melissa suddenly became very interested in her phone, and Felix murmured something about the loo and slipped away.

Alex sent me a don't-worry-look. "Elise, I told you Kate had to wrap up things in L.A. She couldn't get here before today." His voice was mild.

Elise looked up suddenly. "Yes, how is L.A.?" Her mouth pinched, deepening the lines around her lips. "Still sunny and hot and filled with artificial people?" Her clear gray eyes fringed with stubby lashes focused on me for the first time.

"It's very plastic-y at times, yes." I had that wary and unprepared feeling I got when I dreamed that I was back in grad school and arrived at class only to realize it was the day of the final, and I'd forgotten to attend all semester.

She studied me a moment more, and I wondered if I had enough of a balance on my credit card to cover a return ticket to L.A., but then the corners of her mouth turned up in a brief, insincere smile. "You can start with this." She handed me a folder. "Lilac Cottage."

Alex rested his arm on the table. "Kate probably wants to get settled in. She hasn't even been to her room yet." A trace of censure laced through Alex's words.

It was nice he was standing up for me, but I didn't need him to do that.

"No, it's okay." I took the folder. "I got some sleep on the plane. What do you need?" I was obviously on trial, and I wasn't about to give Elise any ammunition to use against me.

"Full scouting report. Can we use it for one of the interviews?" She paused to consult her paper. "One of the scholars—I forget which one, lives there and said it would be most convenient."

I opened the folder. "Rafe Farraday," I read.

At my tone, Alex tilted his head. "Do you know him?"

I slapped the folder closed. "No. Not personally. I know of him. He's quite the online celebrity."

"Really?"

"Yes. He teaches several popular Internet classes."

"That's right," Elise said. "The good-looking one with the following. Personable, funny, and the camera loves him. Yes, thank God we got him. We don't want to lose him. He's the one with the exclusive material, which we've used as a spine for the first episode. Do everything you can to make that location work. We want to keep him happy."

"Of course. When do you want the report?"

Elise looked at me as if I'd grown a third eye. "As soon as possible." Her phone rang, and she picked it up, but didn't answer it. "I understand you worked for Kevin Dunn." Her phone continued to shrill as she said, "I don't know what kind of work environment he allowed—lax, I imagine—but you'll find we do things efficiently and professionally." She nodded once, a dismissal, and answered her call.

Despite feeling like I'd been gutted, I pinned a smile on my face. Defending Kevin would do me no good here. Melissa sent me a sympathetic look. "Call me when you're settled in. We'll get a drink."

"Thanks, I'd like that." I glanced at Alex. "Right now, I think I'll check in and then get started." My blood thumped quickly through my veins, and I knew the best thing would be for me to leave while I could still keep my thoughts to myself.

"I'll help you with your luggage." Alex followed me out of the restaurant portion of the inn to the tall check-in desk. "I'm sorry about that. Elise isn't usually so snappish. It's this weather —we were supposed to start filming. The weather looked great up until the last minute, and we don't have any rain cover for today. We've had to reschedule everything. It's been a nightmare."

"Is it just me she hates or all people from L.A.?"

"She doesn't hate you."

"Could have fooled me."

"Seriously, she's stressed, and she took it out on you. I'm sorry about that. We *do* need you here."

"It's not your fault." I was calming down—that instinctive fight or flight impulse was fading, and I said with a grin, "Wait. Yes, it is. You got me this job."

"Guilty. Don't worry about Elise. It takes her a little while to warm up to people."

"I'm not sure about that. And what was that dig about Kevin? He was a great boss, one of the nicest people out there—and completely professional."

Alex shrugged. "I have no idea. Maybe they knew each other."

A pair of feet appeared, trotting down the stairs, then the stocky, bulldog-like body of Doug Owens, the owner of the inn, came into view. "Ms. Sharp, welcome back."

"Thank you, but please call me Kate."

He came down the last of the steps and paused, his hand resting on the newel post. "I've got some bad news about your room."

Most of the cast and crew were staying at a golf resort in the nearby town of Upper Benning, but the resort was full, so Alex had booked me a room at the Old Nether Woodsmoor Inn.

I squinted. "There was a mistake and you're booked, too?"

"Oh, no. Nothing like that. No, a pipe burst this morning in the room above yours. Water came through the ceiling and everything is soaked. Bed, carpets, furniture. Everything. It will be several days before it's habitable again."

"Oh. Well. Surely there's an open room somewhere close. If not here, then another village nearby. Looks like I'll have to rent a car after all," I said with a glance at Alex.

Doug shook his big head, looking like a groggy dog waking up after a nap. "No. Everything's booked for miles around. I've gotten calls yesterday and today from other villages checking to see if we had openings because they're full up. High season, you know. Everyone wants to get out of the city and enjoy the beautiful countryside."

A crack of thunder made us all jump. We exchanged rueful smiles.

Alex shifted his feet. "I don't have much room, but you're welcome to stay with me. I'll take the couch."

"Oh I couldn't put you out like that," I said quickly. I didn't even have to think about it. I *really* couldn't do that. I wasn't exactly sure where Alex and I stood. We were business associates, of course, but there was something else, an undercurrent that I felt and had fought against during the last time I was in England. I never mixed business with pleasure. I had rules about dating guys I worked with—well, one rule: don't do it. But since Alex had called and pitched the job working with him, I'd been reconsidering my hard and fast rule. Not that I was sure that what Alex and I had would lead to anything romantic...we certainly got on well—aside from our little tiff about the rental car—but maybe it would turn out as more of a friendship thing. One thing I knew for certain was that moving in with him would not help me sort out what was going on.

Doug's glance pinged back and forth between us, and he must have sensed that I wasn't waiting to be talked into staying with Alex because he clapped his hands together. "In that case, I may have a solution." A sharp, high-pitched sound penetrated the din coming from the restaurant "Here it comes now."

The piercing sound continued and resolved itself into a series of sharp dog barks. The yipping increased in volume and cadence as the door to the inn opened, and Beatrice Stone stepped inside, her short pale brown hair plastered to her forehead. Two mops of fur laced in and around her yellow galoshes, then strained at their leashes and raced toward us.

"Kate, I knew you'd be back." Beatrice's square, rather plain face had a smile of welcome on it.

I'd met Beatrice during my first visit and realized that despite her brusque and to-the-point manner, she genuinely cared about the people who lived in the village. In her role as Lady Stone, wife of Sir Harold, a baronet, she looked out for everyone in Nether Woodsmoor as well as she could. She and Sir Harold lived in Parkview Hall, the local "old pile" as Alex called it, a huge country estate with elegant Georgian lines—columned portico, miles of exquisite rooms and galleries, all set in beautiful, naturally landscaped grounds. It had gone to the top of our scouting list as our number one choice for Pemberley when we'd been looking for movie locations, and Alex had said it was now to play the same role for the documentary that would recreate some scenes from Austen's books.

Beatrice reeled in the leashes, pulling the dogs' muddy paws away from our shins. "I hear you need a place to stay, Kate. You're welcome to Honeysuckle Cottage. It's not much to look at, at the moment, but it's dry and has clean linen."

"I'll take it."

"You better see it first."

CHAPTER 2

"WE WERE SCHEDULED TO BEGIN refurbishing it this week," Beatrice said as we splashed along the high street, our individual umbrellas jouncing against each other. The dogs raced ahead, straining at the leashes as if a steak awaited them at the end of their walk. I noticed that the few other pedestrians gave us a wide berth. We must have been quite a sight. Beatrice's trench coat flapped wildly in the wind as she juggled the umbrella, the dog leashes, and a basket with her shopping tucked into one elbow. I huffed along beside her, my suitcase bumping unsteadily over the stone sidewalk and kicking up a spray of water. "But of course the builder called this morning. Unavoidable delay or some such nonsense. Turn here."

She clicked her tongue and the dogs surged up the incline of a short street lined with a few homes, then we turned again and were on a short lane that ran parallel to the high street with seven or eight stone cottages, each with a small front garden. The lane was slightly elevated above the high street and there were no houses on the other side, so the cottages had a view of the village. Behind them, the ground rose, and a grove of trees marched up the knoll, masking a larger house higher on the hill. I could see gables and a chimney through the treetops.

Beatrice pointed to the cottage farthest away at the end of the lane where the pavement transitioned to a small footpath that disappeared into a thicket of trees and underbrush. "Alex lives down here on the end in Ivy Cottage. He took it as a temporary rental, but it's worked into a permanent arrangement. All the cottages are named after plants...Rose, Ivy, Honeysuckle, and so forth. The street is called—rather unimaginatively, I'm afraid—Cottage Lane."

Beatrice opened the fifth gate set in the dry stone wall that fronted all the cottages. Like most of the rock walls in this part of England, it was made without mortar. Flat stones were stacked together in an interlocking pattern with several of the heaviest stones placed on top to hold the whole thing in place. I could just make out the worn inscription posted by the gate that read HONEYSUCKLE COTTAGE.

With the two dogs pulling us forward like they were dragging a sled through the Arctic Circle, we crossed a short stone path and went up the three steps. It took Beatrice a few moments of jiggling the key in the lock, then she threw open the door and commanded the dogs to stay. They promptly circled around the mostly bare room, sniffing and leaving wet paw prints on the dusty hardwood floors as we deposited our umbrellas and my suitcase in a corner.

"We won't have a moment of peace with them in here. Out with you." She unhooked their leashes and pointed to a hallway that led to the back of the cottage. With a symphony of yips accompanied by clattering nails, the dogs disappeared. I heard a door open and close and then there was silence.

The front door opened into a hallway that ran past stairs to a kitchen. On my right was a small living area with a window that overlooked the front garden. A fireplace bracketed with bookshelves filled the wall opposite the window. Wood beams marched across the ceiling and matched the rich wood of the staircase that lined the short hallway. Dust cloths swaddled three pieces of furniture. I pulled them back and found a sixties-inspired angular couch in white fake leather balanced on angled silver legs, a plastic coffee table, also in white, and a plastic chair shaped like a teardrop with a stingy little cushion on the seat.

"Awful, isn't it?" Beatrice stood in the hallway, her arms crossed, the basket still on her elbow.

I let out a laugh. "I didn't want to be rude, but yes, it's terrible. The furniture doesn't go at all."

Beatrice shrugged. "The last tenant had us move the furniture out—it *was* old. Sagging armchairs, chintz couch, a scarred wooden desk, that sort of thing. Wanted to bring in her own furniture, but apparently she wasn't extremely fond of her things either since she moved out and left them all here. Hers was supposed to be a long lease—at least a year, but she only lasted a month."

I sighed, picturing the cottage with the furnishings Beatrice had described. "I bet what you had was perfect."

"Not perfect, but it did match the cottage—in need of a facelift. That's why we scheduled the remodel."

"What are you going to do?"

"Refinish the hardwood floors, fresh paint, new fixtures in the kitchen and bath upstairs—it's only got one bedroom and a small shower—and add a free-standing closet upstairs. It will be a bit of a squeeze, but I think we can do it. Mostly, we're freshening up the place to make it look like a cottage that a Londoner would rent for a holiday in the country. We've done two of the cottages on this lane so far."

"So you own all the cottages?"

"Yes. The first four are for staff from Parkview Hall. We're gradually updating the others as people come and go, converting them to holiday rentals, part of my campaign to make every part of the Hall pay its way." She scanned the beams on the ceiling, and I heard a note of something in her voice that made me tilt my head. "Not everyone likes the plan?"

"No. Some of the staff are very put out. Years ago, if you worked at the Hall, you were provided a place to live along with the salary, but things are changing. The small cottages won't work for most of the staff now. Families are too big for these cottages, and people are more independent. They want to make their own choices. But of course, not everyone sees it that way. Some people feel they've been short-shifted." She sighed. "But we have to do what we must to keep Parkview Hall open."

"Well, I'm glad you have some of them as rentals. Despite the furniture, it's lovely."

"You'd best see the kitchen and bath before you give your final verdict."

I followed her down the narrow hallway. "Bit of storage in here." Beatrice tapped a small door set into the wall under the stairs. A large hutch with drawers and shelves dominated the tiny kitchen. There was barely enough room for Beatrice and me to stand together in the kitchen. It had been updated at least once, probably sometime shortly after World War II. Everything was miniaturized—the sink, the two-burner stove, and the rounded refrigerator looked like something from Barbie's dream home circa 1950. The prior tenant's furniture updating spree hadn't extended to the kitchen. A heavy round table wedged into one corner, its top burnished from years of use, matched the solid hutch.

"It's workable for one. I'm not much of a cook actually, so it will be fine for me."

Beatrice nodded, and I followed her up the stairs, which opened directly into a room with a brass bed centered below a steep A-line roof with heavy beams interspersed between a whitewashed ceiling. "The former tenant didn't love the bed frame, but getting it down the narrow stairs was too much for her." Beatrice moved to the window and opened a set of interior shutters.

"Well, I think it's perfect." A white bedspread with swirls of embroidery covered the bed. Pillows with a honeysuckle print fabric were propped up against the headboard. The only other furniture was a bedside table with a lamp. A curtain in the same honeysuckle fabric angled across one corner. I pulled it away to reveal a self-standing IKEA storage unit with shelves and a tiny rod for hanging clothes.

I poked my head into the bath. A row of accent tiles in Pepto-Bismol pink cut through octagonal tiles in black and white that lined the room, which had a pedestal sink and a toilet with a pull chain. I was relieved to see a fairly modern shower insert.

"I love it."

"I'll delay the renovation until after your show...what do you call it...ends?"

"Wraps."

"Yes, until you wrap. I doubt it will make much of a difference in the remodeling completion date. The builder seems the unreliable type, cancelling on the first day of a job." Beatrice spoke over her shoulder as she carefully maneuvered down the stairs. I followed her.

She named a sum for a weekly rental that I thought was more than fair, considering what the weekly rate at the Old Nether Woodsmoor Inn would have been. I knew the production would cover it and be happy about the savings, so I said, "I'll take it. I'll talk to Elise about the payment of the rent."

She waved away my concern as she picked up her umbrella. "I'll have one of those nice P.A. people add it to the production's bill." She worked two oversized old-fashioned keys off her keychain. "Excellent to have you back in town, Kate. Take these for the night latch locks. Front and back door."

"Night latch?"

"Come see," she said, and I followed her into the kitchen where she paused by the door that led into the small back garden. "This lock." She twisted a knob secured to a rectangular piece of metal attached to both the door and the frame. "It's a spring bolt that locks automatically when the door closes. It opens with the key from the outside."

"I see. Sort of a deadbolt. But shouldn't you keep these? Aren't these your own set?"

"No, I have another copy back at the Hall. And the keys to the cottages that haven't been renovated are practically interchangeable in a pinch anyway. You looked shocked, which is perfectly natural, you coming from the city, but it's not common knowledge, and it only works if you jiggle the key about in the lock quite a bit." She tapped a sliding bolt at shoulder height on the door. "Use this when you're in at night. There's one on the front door as well. Normally, I wouldn't even tell you to use the bolt, but well," she shook her head and pressed her lips together before continuing, "lately, our little village has had a rash of vandalism."

"What's happened?"

"Nothing serious. Just a few broken windows here and there. A car scratched up all along the side."

"Keyed, you mean?"

"Yes, that's what Constable Albertson called it. Such a shame. But things always get a bit wilder during the summer season. All the visitors, you know."

"And the production company is here as well. Anyone blaming the incidents on them?"

"Not that I've heard. Everyone is thrilled to pieces with the attention, as far as I can tell. We're the envy of every hamlet for miles around, even if we don't have any Hollywood stars here."

I had to smile. The documentary was quite a step down from the feature film production. There were no big names attached to the current project, except for Elise DuPont. She was famous in some Hollywood circles for her documentaries, but she certainly wasn't a household name who turned up in the tabloids.

"I'll let you get settled in. There's a grocery at the end of high street where you can get some nice veg. Farmer's Market every Friday. Better produce there. And there's a nice fish and chips takeaway on your left when you cross over the high street. Can't miss it." She opened the door and the dogs surged toward her, yapping joyfully. She petted them both as she snapped on their leashes then headed up a narrow path to a back gate in another stone wall. The rain had stopped, but dark clouds still hung low.

A couple on bikes, their waterproof jackets glowing brightly in the dimness of the overcast day, flew by along the stone wall at the back of the garden. Another single walker in a tangerine jacket strode along behind them. "Is there another road behind the cottages?"

"No, it's a footpath." She frowned after the bikers. "It's not wide enough for bikers and ramblers, but these summer people ignore the posted signs. The footpath starts down in the village and curves around here then continues up the hill to a fork. The right fork takes you up to Tate House." She pointed through the treetops at the gables. "The left fork takes you down to the river. Drops you near the Parkview Hall bridge—" she broke off, obviously remembering what had happened at that bridge. "I'm sorry."

"No, it's fine. I love to walk, and the bridge is a beautiful area. I'm sure I'll go that way someday."

"Stop in and say hello when you do."

"I'll do that."

"Don't worry about the garden." She gestured at the many rosebushes, climbing vines, and flowerbeds. "The gardener comes one day a week. He does all the holiday rentals."

I nodded an acknowledgement, glad that I wasn't responsible for the lush plantings. I love the English garden look, but the extent of my gardening experience was limited to an ivy plant that I had kept on my desk at work. I half-closed the door, then stepped back outside.

"Is Lilac Cottage close?"

She pointed to the row of tall yews that lined each side of the small yard, separating the properties. "Right next door."

CHAPTER 3

*A*FTER BEATRICE LEFT, I MANEUVERED my suitcase upstairs and unpacked, which didn't take long. I'd always traveled light and even though I knew I was going to be in England for an extended amount of time, I couldn't break the habit of only bringing the bare minimum. I'd compensated for this quirk by stuffing two cardboard boxes full of clothes and mailing them to the inn. I knew that even though I wasn't staying there, Doug would call me as soon as they arrived.

I hung up my last shirt and headed for the shower to freshen up. I learned that just because something *looks* like it has been updated doesn't mean it has been. The shower had all the water pressure of a garden hose trapped under a car tire. The trickle of water was at least clear and warm. I slipped on fresh clothes, added some makeup to cover the circles under my eyes, and brushed my hair up into a neater ponytail before calling Alex.

The call went straight to his voicemail, so I told him my room situation was sorted, and he could find me at Honeysuckle Cottage. I sent a quick text to Marci. *Things are looking up. I'm staying in an English cottage. Too quaint for words.* I finished the message with a smiley face then scanned the cozy room. *All mine,* at least for a few weeks, I thought. The boss situation might not be exactly what I would have picked, but the living quarters, despite the modern furniture downstairs, were all that I could have hoped for.

I wrangled the suitcase back down the stairs and stowed it in the closet under the stairs. I dialed the phone number listed in Rafe Farraday's file and listened to it ring. When it clicked over to his voicemail, I said, "Hello, my name is Kate Sharp. I am a location scout working with the Jane Austen documentary production, and I need to meet with you as soon as possible, preferably at your cottage. Please give me a call back. Thanks."

I hung up and skimmed the rest of the file, not expecting to find anything I didn't know. During my short-lived expedition to graduate school, I'd heard about Rafe Farraday. An untenured professor at a nearby university in Southern California, his online course on the introduction to the English novel hit at just the right time when online courses were gaining in popularity and expanding the reach of college education far beyond colleges' typical geographic boundaries.

Excerpts of his witty lectures were posted around the Internet where they went viral. Not viral in a *Call Me Maybe* kind of way, but viral for the academic world. From Southern California to the Ivy League, Rafe Farraday was the talk of English departments—both among the professors and the students. He was a star on the rise, one of a handful of celebrity professors who drew publicity to their university and boosted enrollment because of their charismatic personalities. He'd written many articles and been published in several peer reviewed journals. It was no surprise that he'd been offered a tenured position at his university.

I tried to read through the file with an objective eye, but it was hard to ignore the whisper in the back of my mind saying *that could have been you.* If things had worked out differently, if I hadn't had to drop out of the program, if I could have scraped up the money to re-enroll...I could be teaching students about Jane Austen, writing papers about her life and books...

I shook my head, moving on to the next page of information. I couldn't change the past. I had to keep moving forward from where I was. I paused over the last bit of information in the file. Rafe Farraday had written a book analyzing the popularity of Jane Austen and how her fame had changed over time. I wasn't up on all the latest Jane Austen studies and wasn't aware of his book, or that he was currently on sabbatical, working on another book that was under contract.

I closed the file then gathered up my Moleskine notebook, my camera, extra memory cards and batteries, as well as my cell phone and the set of keys to the cottage. After jiggling the key in the lock on the front door for quite a bit longer than Beatrice had, I finally managed to lock the door from the outside. I walked down the front path, took a right, and entered the gate of the cottage next door. I walked up three steps and rang the bell. Elise didn't seem to be the sort of person who'd take it well if I said I'd called Rafe Farraday and sat around waiting for his return call. I pressed the bell again.

After a long pause, the door jerked open. "Yes?" Rafe Farraday said with a slightly annoyed expression raising his already peaked eyebrows. Instead of wearing a button down shirt, blazer, and no tie, his usual teaching attire that I'd seen on his videos, he had on a T-shirt with an In-An-Out burger logo, worn jeans, and sandals. He held a piece of board cut into a square in one hand.

"Sorry to bother you," I said, jumping in with my brightest smile. "I'm Kate Sharp. I called you earlier—"

"About five minutes ago." He had an expressive face, something that I remembered from watching a few of his lectures online. It wasn't only what he said in class that made an impact, but the expressions he used as he worked through a text or discussed ideas—a grimace or a mocking shudder or surprise— all conveyed with a comedian's impeccable timing, that was the main thing that stood out in my memory of his talks. Now his pointy brows were flattened into an impatient frown.

"Yes. Sorry for the intrusion, but the producer really wants to nail down locations for your interview, and since I'm staying next door," I glanced at Honeysuckle Cottage, "I thought I'd just run over on the off-chance that you might be home."

"How long will this take?"

"Not long. I only need to get some photos and make a few notes."

He opened the door wider. "Fine, I'll let you in since you're a fellow American—it's nice to hear someone without a British accent—but you'll have to help me first. I could use an extra pair of hands."

"Okay." I walked into the cottage. The design was identical to mine down to the storage space under the stairs. I only had a quick glimpse of the living area at the front of the house, but it was obvious that Rafe's cottage hadn't been renovated or updated either. The shabby chic chintz armchairs by the fireplace and the ornately carved desk looked worn and well used. The kitchen looked like mine as well with the same layout and similarly aged appliances.

He went straight to the back door, which had a glass insert in the upper half. Two panes of glass on the bottom were broken out. "Watch where you step." He gestured to a dustpan full of glass shards and a broom leaning against the counter.

"What happened?"

"Kids, I imagine."

"Someone broke in?" I surveyed the empty panes. Once broken, it would be easy to reach inside and turn the knob on the night latch or unlock the sliding bolt that was positioned higher on the door.

"No, the door wasn't even opened."

"Well, that's good, I guess. Although, I'm having serious doubts about the neighborhood I just moved into."

Rafe grinned. "It's a one time thing. Nothing to worry about."

"Really? I heard there was some vandalism of cars as well."

"Hmm. Didn't know about that. Anyway, I wouldn't worry about it. If someone wanted to rob a house, I doubt that they'd pick these cottages. Tate House would be a much better target. The most valuable thing I've got in here is my copy of *The Great Gatsby*." He held up the board so that it covered the empty panes. "Would you mind holding this while I drill it into place?"

"Sure." I held the board while he produced an electric screwdriver and efficiently buzzed the screws into place. "There. Thank you very much."

"So you have to do your own repairs?"

"No, the maintenance crew from Parkview Hall is quite good at taking care of things, but I don't mind doing it myself, at least a temporary repair, to help out. I put myself through school working in home construction, so I can handle some of the minor things." He wound the cord around the drill, replaced it in a carrying case, and snapped it shut. "They provided the tools and materials, and I put in the elbow grease. Not a bad trade, especially since they're busy repairing several broken windows around the village."

"How many?"

"Five or six that I heard about. Now, how can I help you?"

"I need to take photographs and make some notes for the filming of your interview. You want it to take place in the front room?"

"Yes, in the parlor. It's a perfect setting, don't you think?" He led the way back down the hall.

I surveyed the room with a critical eye. "It is small, but considering it will be an interview, I think it will work. And the shelves of books on either side of the fireplace would make a wonderful background. Very professorial."

"Great. What do I need to do? Clean up?" He moved toward the desk, which had a scattering of papers and books splayed open and stacked on each other with sticky notes protruding from their edges. He moved a leather messenger bag off the desk, revealing a laptop computer. I noticed it was a slim, expensive model in shiny silver. He did have something that would be fairly valuable to steal. He hung the messenger bag on the back of the chair and straightened some books.

"Nothing. It's fine. This assessment looks at the big picture. If we need to make any changes, the set dressers will see to that, but everything will be photographed and then put back exactly as it was before." In theory that was what was supposed to happen. In practice...well, it depended on the thoroughness of the location manager. I kept those thoughts to myself, knowing that Alex or I would make sure everything was perfectly replaced before we left.

I took my camera out of my tote and photographed the room from several angles then checked the compass app on my phone and jotted down the position of the room along with notes about the quality of the light.

The camera does funny things to people. Rafe Farraday wasn't what I thought of as traditionally handsome, but he had nice, regular features, brownish-blond hair, and a normal physique. He wasn't extremely broad shouldered or extra lean—just your average joe. Maybe that was part of the reason for his popularity. Some people become introverts when a camera appears, closing off from the lens, while others react in the opposite way, opening up in a way that instinctively draws viewers to them. They have that sparkling of pixie dust, the elusive *it* factor, that either you possess or you don't. Rafe Farraday had it, and when the camera came out, it was as if someone had flipped a switch. His face became even more animated as he settled on the corner of the desk, one leg swinging jauntily as he reached for a pair of glasses and settled them on his nose. "Scholarly enough for the masses?"

"Replace the In-and-Out Burger T-shirt with a tweedy, elbow-patched jacket and I think you're almost there."

"These are just for show anyway."

"Why do you need them here? No students or faculty to impress here."

He shrugged. "Some habits are hard to break. I picked up a pair of clear lens glasses when I started as a teaching assistant. I wanted to be taken seriously. Sometimes it's the appearance more than the substance that matters, especially in this new media age." He tossed the glasses back on the desktop and moved around to the chair where he began to sort and stack papers. "Let me know if you need anything from me."

I took measurements, made my notes in my Moleskine notebook, and snapped a few more pictures. I moved to the desk. "That should do it, Mr. Farraday."

"Call me Rafe."

"Rafe, then. Thank you so much for your—" I broke off as I noticed a familiar blue spine with white lettering under a spray of papers. "Is that your copy of *The Great Gatsby?*"

"Yes, indeed." Rafe shoved the papers aside, revealing the famous cover illustration of sad eyes over a bright landscape. The cover, which had a few rips and gouges, was encased in a sleeve of plastic. He handed it to me.

"I love this cover." I studied it a moment then flipped to the book description on the back. In the center of the text, the first letter of the name "Jay" was darker than the rest of the printing. I ran my finger lightly over the plastic cover then paused with my index finger at the corrected capital letter. "First edition," I breathed.

"You know your stuff," Rafe said, his tone more respectful than it had been.

"I did some graduate work in English Lit." I handed the book back. "This is valuable. If vandals knew it was here…"

He shook his head and flicked through the pages. "I doubt someone who throws stones to break windows would recognize the monetary worth of this. Besides, it's not a first-rate example."

He pointed out the scuffs and dings on the cover as well as several pen marks inside. "As an English grad student, you'll appreciate this." He turned to a page and pointed to a line of text that read "sick in tired."

"One of the many typos," he said with a grin. "Makes me feel better to know that the great F. Scott didn't proofread perfectly either. I know it would be smarter to have it hidden away in a bank vault somewhere, but books were meant to be read and talked about, not tucked away." He turned and placed it in an open slot on the bookshelf among John le Carré and Robert Ludlum books. "Besides, I pull it out when I get a particularly scathing one-star review. Helps me keep it all in perspective. Couldn't do that if it was locked in a vault."

He leaned a shoulder against the bookcase. "So you were a grad student. What was your area of study?"

"I was always partial to Jane Austen."

"Good choice."

I tilted my head. "So you have some exclusive material about Jane Austen?"

He frowned. "Where did you hear that?"

"Production company chatter."

He stepped away from the shelves, his manner frosty. "I can't talk about it. I'm sure you understand. A word here, a word there, and then it's not exclusive anymore. But back to you. So what happened?"

"What do you mean?"

"You were a grad student. Did you graduate? Do you teach? What happened?"

"Life got in the way." I gave him a quick smile and moved to the door. "Thanks so much for your time. The production will get in touch with you with details about the interview."

The rain had started up again. I hurried down the steps and scurried to my cottage where I again struggled with the lock until it finally opened.

I DOWNLOADED the photos of Rafe's cottage, selecting the best ones, then resized them and compiled a written scouting report for Elise. I called her, asking how she wanted to receive it. "Email it, of course," she snapped. "And in the future, call Mary, my P.A., with trivial questions like that." She hung up and a few seconds later, I received a text from her. *I need you at Parkview tomorrow at five sharp. Talk to Alex. He has all the details.*

I assumed that it was actually Mary's email that she wanted the report sent to, but Elise hadn't given me either Mary's email or her own, so I called Alex.

"Do you have an email address for Elise's P.A.?"

"Yes, let me send it to you."

"Great. Send me Elise's as well. And anyone else's that you think would be useful."

"I'll send them as soon as we hang up. Were you able to look at the cottage Elise wanted you to scout?"

"Yes. Report's done. That's why I need the emails."

"Elise will be impressed. I told her you were top-notch."

"She didn't sound impressed."

"Well, she's not going to come out and say it. That might ruin her image."

"No danger of that," I said. "So Parkview Hall tomorrow? Elise says you'll give me all the details."

"Right. How about we meet at the pub in an hour? We can discuss it over dinner."

"Sounds good."

A long text came in a few minutes later with what must have been contact information for most of the crew and local people associated with the production. I sent off the report to Mary, but made sure to copy Elise on it. I didn't want any confusion on whether or not I'd completed the assignments she'd given me. Then I set two alarms, made up the bed with a stack of fresh linen from the little makeshift closet, and allowed myself to stretch out on the bed and close my eyes.

~

THE WHITE DUCK pub was even noisier and more crowded than the inn's restaurant had been earlier in the day. Alex saw me and half stood. I made my way through the evening crowd to his table. Louise, the owner of the pub, saw me and gave an exaggerated wave that shook her cherry black ponytail. She performed a mime, indicating she was drowning in orders, and I called out that I would talk with her later. I was glad she was busy. At least the stormy weather would help her business.

Alex didn't meet me halfway or give me a one-arm hug, which was fine. I hadn't been expecting either one...had I? No, of course not. I reached the corner booth where Alex and Melissa Millbank were seated. Another man stood beside the table holding a plastic bag of take-out food boxed in Styrofoam containers. Light blond hair brushed the frames of his wire-rimmed glasses. He had a blond beard and mustache threaded with a few hints of gray and wore a black raincoat over a beige shirt and dark pants.

"Kate, this is Hector Lyons, our elusive neighbor," Alex said.

I extended my hand and worked a smile onto my face. It had been a long day and even though it was early—barely after six, I was feeling every minute of the time change. My nap was just long enough that my body clock was thoroughly confused.

"Elusive neighbor?" I asked as we shook hands.

"Hector lives in Tate House. You can see his roof through the trees on the hill above the cottages."

"Oh, yes. Beatrice pointed it out."

"And he's there...well, pretty much all the time," Alex explained.

"Not all the time. I'm here, aren't I?" Hector shook his head, but was already backing away from the table, clearly intent on leaving the little group as soon as he could.

"But you're already heading back. You've been out, what, thirty minutes at the most, I bet," Alex said.

"What can I say? A computer programmer's work is never done." He rapped lightly on the table with a knuckle, nodded to me and moved swiftly through the tables.

Alex waved me into the booth ahead of him, so I scooted around to sit between him and Melissa, who asked, "So, he works out of his home? Must be a pretty good job if he can afford that house on the hill."

Alex said, "I have no idea who he works for. He's freelance, I think. He's never really said, but he's always busy so he must be in demand. I never would have met him if he hadn't joined the cycling club and gone on a few rides with us."

"I didn't know you cycled," I said.

"You sound astonished."

"No, not that you ride. It just seems that bicycling would be a little…tame…for you." I could easily picture Alex's lean form on a bike, but I knew he was once very big into snowboarding.

"Our cycling club certainly isn't the Tour de France, but we do some challenging rides occasionally. Most of the time it is just about enjoying the countryside and getting some exercise."

"Sounds fun," I said. "I haven't ridden a bike in years."

"You should join us. We have a ride this coming Saturday. It's a scheduled day off from filming. Nothing competitive like the last one. It was a three-tiered race last week, so this next one is relaxed."

"Three-tiered?"

"Different divisions. We had a 40-mile route as well as a 75- and 100-mile route."

I raised my eyebrows. "One hundred miles? On a bike? Okay, I take back what I said about it being too tame. I'm not signing up for anything like that, am I?"

"No, next week is a short one, three kilometers. That's about two miles. We're going out to Bradley Castle. It's a ruin. You'd like it, I think. Very *Northanger Abbey*. Or, at least, that's what it makes me think of now that I've read it."

"You've read *Northanger Abbey*?" I asked. When I met Alex, we'd chatted about Jane Austen books, and he'd told me he'd only read *Pride and Prejudice* in school, but had reread it before starting work on the film.

"You said it was one of your favorites," he said simply. "Seemed a good book to go on to after *P & P*."

"Hmm." I looked down at the table, not sure what to say. I'd never had a guy read a book I'd mentioned.

"So, would you like to see it?" Alex asked.

"What?"

"Bradley Castle."

"Oh, yes. Definitely. But I'm not sure about two miles as a starting point for my first bike ride. I might need to work up to that."

"Don't do much biking around Hollywood?" His tone was teasing, not critical.

"No. The gridlock on the freeways makes it impossible." I looked around the crowded pub to the quiet street through the rain-streaked window. "That's why I came here."

Alex smiled slowly at me, which for some reason made my insides go rather mushy. I looked away and caught Melissa's gaze bouncing back and forth between us. She grinned quickly at me, then looked toward the window where Hector's fuzzy outline went by, his shoulders hunched against the rain.

"So he's not a joiner?" Melissa asked.

"Who?" Alex asked as he pulled his gaze away from me.

"Hector."

"No. Far from it. If he didn't cycle, I probably never would have met him."

"Is he married?"

"I don't know." Alex shrugged. "I don't think so. I haven't seen a woman around, and he's never mentioned his wife, but he's not talkative."

"Interesting," Melissa said as she stared at the rainy window.

"How about some food?" Alex asked. We decided on fish and chips for all of us, and Alex left to turn in our order at the bar.

As he walked away, Melissa sighed. "You're lucky. He's sweet."

"What?"

"Oh, don't pretend. After five seconds around you both, I can tell he likes you. He read a book for you," she said, her tone awed. "That's impressive."

"And a nineteenth century novel, at that."

Melissa nodded. "Yep. I can hardly get some guys to read my texts. He's into you. And," she studied my face for a moment, "right. You like him, too. Okay, then. He was too good for me anyway." She tilted her head and looked across the room for a moment. "Or, more likely, I'm too bad for him," she said with a wicked grin. "It looks like I need to find a reason to either cycle," she shuddered, "or perhaps I'll have a little computer problem." She nodded. "Yeah, I like that one much better."

"You want to get to know Hector better?" I asked, surprised that Melissa had even given the guy a second look. "He seemed kind of," I glanced up at her bright bangs and brow rings, "bland for you."

"Well, he's obviously got something going for him if he lives in that big house on the hill. Have you seen that place?"

"Only the roof."

"It's huge."

"So Hector is the best prospect around here? Aren't there any other guys on the crew or in the village?"

"In the crew? No, Alex is the best of that lot. Everyone else is either married or way below my standards, and the only eligible bachelor in the village is that egotistical scholar twit."

"Rafe Farraday?"

"Yeah, him."

"Really? You thought he was a twit? He was very nice to me today. Well, most of the time," I amended, thinking of his impatience when he opened the door.

"Well, you speak his language. You know all about Jane Austen and books and *literature*." She used a super-posh accent when she said the word *literature*, managing to sound both snotty and affected. "Besides, you were scouting the location, right?"

"Yes." She lifted a shoulder. "He needs something from you. Of course he's going to be nice to you. Once he gets it, then forget it." I shifted uncomfortably in my seat, not sure what to say. "He's very friendly with Becca Ford," Melissa added.

"Oh." My opinion of Rafe Farraday nose-dived.

"You know her?"

"I met her when I was here last time." Beautiful, wealthy, bored, pretentious, and interested in any man within a ten-yard radius about summed her up. I knew that Becca was married, but from what I'd heard, her banker husband rarely made the trip to Nether Woodsmoor. Apparently, he didn't mind—or perhaps care—what Becca did in the village. "We didn't get on well." Especially after I pointed a murder investigation in her direction.

Alex returned to the table and our conversation turned to work. When our food arrived, I pulled my plate toward me, but said, "My body clock is messed up from the time change. It doesn't feel like dinner time."

"I don't have that problem. I just eat all the time." Melissa popped a golden strip of fried potato into her mouth.

I swiveled toward Alex. "Tell me about Rafe. What's this exclusive thing that Elise mentioned earlier? I asked him about it, but he wouldn't tell me anything."

Alex glanced at Melissa. "Have you heard?"

"About the letters? Oh, yeah," she said, her tone casual.

Alex leaned back. "Then I guess we can discuss it freely."

Melissa held her fish delicately by her fingertips. "There are no secrets on the set. I don't know why he thinks he can keep it quiet."

"What letters?" I asked, picking up my fish. It was so hot that I dropped it.

"Jane Austen's lost letters. You know, the juicy ones," Melissa said.

"What?" I turned toward her, my food forgotten. "There are no lost Austen letters. Her sister Cassandra destroyed most of her correspondence."

Melissa licked her fingertips. "Well, Rafe says he has some."

I looked to Alex, who nodded. "The details were in the preproduction paperwork. He says he found them in a little village in Hampshire."

"Was it Chawton? That's where Austen and her sister lived during the last years of their lives."

"No," Alex said. "Somewhere else. Can't remember the name. Anyway, says he bought the letters from some old woman who claimed she was descended from Austen's niece, that they'd been handed down for generations and kept private, but the woman had fallen on hard times and needed to sell them, paid through the nose for them, apparently."

"That's crazy. It has to be a hoax. There's no way a letter—let alone many letters—from Jane Austen would have gone undiscovered for this long. She's been dead for," I paused, tripping over the mental math, and finally said, "nearly two hundred years. She's one of the world's most famous authors. If there were letters, they would have been found by now."

Alex grinned. "Passionate much?"

"About Austen, yes."

Alex went back to eating. "Well, everything has been verified and authenticated. You know Elise's reputation. She wouldn't go out on a limb for something flim-flammy."

"I don't know. It sounds too good to be true." My fish had cooled enough that I could pick it up.

Melissa wiped her fingers on her napkin. "You know there are all those news stories about lost masterpieces found in attics and garages. It could happen."

"I suppose," I said, already thinking about how I could convince Rafe to let me have a look at the letters.

CHAPTER 4

*T*WO WOMEN IN BONNETS, GLOVES, and high-waisted gowns of sprigged muslin strolled arm-in-arm across the green lawn, the buttery stones of Parkview Hall glowing in the distance behind them. A pair of gentlemen in buff-colored breeches and dark coats with intricate cravats at their necks approached the ladies. Bows and curtsies were exchanged, then the gentlemen offered their arms, and the four people separated into pairs and strolled along the sand path.

If I squinted and focused on the two couples, I could almost ignore the profusion of cameras, the tangle of cords, and the phalanx of people clothed in jeans, wrinkled shirts, and in Melissa's case, a pair of fringed cowboy boots with a matching fringed T-shirt. The mass of people followed the four costumed actors as they promenaded through the lush grounds of Parkview Hall until the word, "Cut!" echoed through the air.

The men in costume immediately ran fingers around their tight cravats, and Melissa sprang into action, fringe flapping, as she noted the position of each person and what each person had been doing during the shot. A woman with a tool-belt like apparatus that bulged with make-up brushes and cosmetics moved between the two Regency-costumed women, touching up their makeup.

The clouds were gone, and the sun was out in full force today. One of my most closely guarded secrets was my desire to dress in Regency appropriate attire—just once. But watching the women in the bright sunlight was making me reconsider. The gloves, the bonnet, not to mention all the layers of fabric, must feel stifling.

I saw Alex walk over the hill from the formal gardens area of the grounds and waved. He was pretty far away, but his longish brown hair and his easy stride were unmistakable. He'd rolled up the sleeves of his pale green oxford shirt to his elbows. He held something in each hand, but he lifted one hand in acknowledgement.

He had walked me home last night from the pub and said a very formal, almost business-like, good-night from the bottom porch step. At the time, I'd been exhausted and hadn't given the interaction more than a passing thought. But now that I wasn't practically sleep-walking, I wondered if I was completely wrong about Alex and the signals I thought he'd been sending me. I couldn't be. That look he'd given me in the pub... I hadn't imagined that. And he'd read *Northanger Abbey*. Maybe he was just being gentlemanly last night. I watched him walk toward me, my head tilted, trying to work it out. Had I actually found a man who behaved in a "gentleman-like manner," as Austen would call it? Did those men exist in the twenty-first century?

He ducked under the branch of a huge oak tree where I was taking a break from the sun and handed me a to-go cup. He had been taking care of a traffic issue—something about a delivery truck that had to get to the house immediately.

Running interference was our main task today. On filming days, our job was to handle any problem that came up. I'd heard some location scouts call themselves fixers, and that was what our job entailed today. I'd already coordinated traffic issues with the local constable, checked the weather multiple times, and soothed an irritated neighbor down the road who hadn't been happy when several people parked in his driveway, attempting to get close to the filming.

"Coffee. Thank you, thank you, thank you." I sipped and sighed blissfully. "Not my normal lunch beverage, but I'm barely keeping my eyes open." Okay, I wasn't sure about the gentleman-like restraint on my doorstep last night, but anyone who brings me coffee goes up in my estimation.

"Yeah. That five a.m. departure was rough," Alex said, running his hand over the layer of stubble on his chin and jaw.

"I figure I'll be living on naps for a few days anyway." Alex had picked me up this morning in his sporty, if slightly creaky, vintage red MG convertible, and we'd put up the signs that directed the cast and crew to the filming location, met with the local constable about traffic issues, and then checked on the outdoor filming location to make sure set-up was going according to plan for filming.

Alex reached in the pocket of his brown cargo pants for his keys. "We're about to break for lunch. I need to go by the house and let Slink out. Want to ride with me?" he asked, referring to his dog, a greyhound with a mostly mellow disposition. "I have Henry—you remember him—Doug's son at the inn? I have him let her out and take her for a run on the days I can't be home or bring her with me, but he can't do it today."

"Sure." I knew Alex sometimes brought Slink when he was scouting locations, but it wouldn't be possible to have her along on a day as busy as this one was.

A few minutes later, I met Alex at his car. I'd been pretty groggy earlier and hadn't done much more than drop into the car seat and work on keeping my eyelids open, but now as I slid into the passenger seat, I noticed that Alex still had an array of sticky notes dotting the dashboard. One of them had my name on it, underlined twice, with my flight number and arrival time.

A haphazardly folded map and a stack of papers were wedged

into the gap between the passenger seat and the console. As Alex backed out, it all tumbled out and fell around my feet. "Sorry about that."

"It's fine." I restacked the paper and was about to put it back, but Alex held out his hand. "Here. Let me get that out of your way."

As he drove with one hand on the wheel, he contorted his other arm around and shoved the pile into the miniscule crevice behind the seats. I glanced back and saw he'd stuffed many items back there. Papers and brochures, an umbrella, a squashed baseball cap, permanent markers, a pad of sticky notes, and a roll of tape were just the things I could see sticking up around the edges. He reached back for the map, which had unfurled when I picked up a corner, but I said, "I don't think there's room for it back there. At least, not in this state."

Alex raised an eyebrow. "Do I detect a note of criticism? You don't approve of my storage system?" he asked, his face serious, but I knew him well enough now to see the tiny upturn of one corner of his mouth.

I smoothed the map across my lap and folded it along the scored lines. "I'm not sure what you have could be called a system. Technically speaking."

"Oh, it's a system. A highly evolved system."

"Really? I wouldn't have thought it. Looks rather haphazard."

"I won't bother to explain it to you. Somehow, I don't think you'd appreciate it."

"Try me."

"I'll only say that I can find anything I want back there within three seconds, but that won't convince you. You'll say it's only luck. You wouldn't be any more impressed with my storage system than I would be with your labels and cross-referencing. Neither one of us will convert the other, so I think we should each stick to our methods and be happy with that."

"Hmm. I do love labels. Actually, I'm a sucker for any office product."

We drove into Nether Woodsmoor, and he took the turn to Cottage Lane. "Good to know the way to your heart lies in staplers and file folders. Probably color-coded file folders, if I had to hazard a guess."

"Guilty. And I don't apologize for it." I folded the last section of the map. "There." I put it back in the gap between the seat and the console. How did Alex and I slip into this banter so effortlessly? I glanced over my shoulder at the disarray stuffed behind the seats then to Alex in his wrinkled and creased oxford with his rumpled hair and stubble. Normally, clean-shaven guys appealed to me, but there was something about Alex's unshaved look that I liked. It seemed masculine. We were so different, but I felt comfortable with him. It was...weird. He was everything I thought I didn't want in a guy, and yet...

He rolled to a stop in front of his cottage. He switched off the car then turned to me, his face serious. "Kate, there's something —" He paused then started again. "I—you see—" He looked away from me and murmured something about getting it over with.

"Um, no, I don't see." I tilted my head, worried because of his serious expression. "What is it?"

He looked down at the map, then sighed. "Nothing." He gave me a quick smile that crinkled the skin around his dark brown eyes. "Do you want to come in?"

"No, I was planning to run back to my cottage and get my sunglasses."

"Right. Yes. Good. I'll meet you back here then? At the car?"

"Yes," I replied, uncertainly. "Where else would I meet you?"

"True. Very true."

I walked to Honeysuckle Cottage. What had just happened? Whatever it was had sucked the easy rapport right out of the atmosphere. I removed my sunglasses from the side pocket in my suitcase—right were I'd packed them. I wondered if Alex could find his as easily. Somehow, I didn't think we'd be bantering about it on the way back.

I heard the tinkling sound of breaking glass as I returned the suitcase to the storage area under the stairs. I paused, listening, but didn't hear anything else. I hurried to the front door and cautiously opened it. Rafe, walking toward a rolling trash bin positioned at the curb, was the only person on the street.

He held a dustpan. "Just a bottle that fell out of the wheelie bin." He angled the dustpan with shards of glass toward me. "Completely my fault," he said. "I wedged it in the side of the bin, but it fell out when I bumped the bin out here to the curb."

"I'm glad it's nothing more serious than that." I glanced up and down the lane again.

"Yes. We're all a little on edge around here."

I nodded then said, "So tomorrow must be trash day." A rolling bin was positioned near the curb in front of each cottage.

"Yes, and they come to empty them at an ungodly hour of the morning. Best have yours out tonight."

"Right. Thanks for the tip. I'm not sure I have anything in mine. In fact, I'm not sure I even *have* a trash bin."

"Oh, I think all the cottages do. Mine was behind a hedge. Yours is probably the same." He pointed to a hedge of about shoulder height that extended in an L-shape at one side of the cottage. I struggled with the lock on my front door until it clicked, then checked the hedge, and emerged with my own bin. It had a bag of trash in it, probably left over from either the last tenant or the cleaning of the cottage after she left. I bumped it down the little path to the curb. "I'm all set now."

"Excellent." Rafe tilted the dustpan, and the glass shards jingled into the bin. He slapped the lid closed. "See you."

"I'd love to see the letters," I called after him. I couldn't let him disappear back inside without at least broaching the subject.

His steps checked, and he looked back over his shoulder. "What letters?"

"The Jane Austen letters."

I think he tried to laugh, but it came out sounding more like he'd choked. "Jane Austen letters? I don't know what you're talking about."

"Sure you do. You can tell me. I'm working for the production company. I'll keep your secret. I'd really love to see the lost Austen letters."

He glanced up and down the street quickly, a horrified look on his face, then he closed the distance between us, coming to stand beside my trash bin. "How did you find out?"

"Word gets around on a set."

Rafe looked skyward. "You've been here less than a day."

"Yes, but I'm interested in Austen. I heard you had some exclusive material, and I asked a few questions. Most people wouldn't do that—or even care, actually." Most people liked Austen's books and the adaptations of her work, but they weren't as enthusiastic as I was.

Rafe put an arm on the lid of the bin and leaned against it. "I was given promises. People signed confidentiality agreements. And they made *me* sign confidentiality agreements. Obviously, I'm not the weak link in the chain when it comes to secrecy."

"It's okay." I put a hand on his arm, envisioning him complaining to Elise, and her blaming his anger on me. "I'm not about to say a word to anyone outside the production, and the people who told me—well, they didn't understand the significance of what you have. I didn't believe them until I saw your reaction."

Rafe let out a snort. "I gave the game away, did I?" His initial anger was gone, and now he sounded dismayed. "That's a lesson for me."

"Can I see them?"

"I don't have them here."

"But they'll need to be filmed for the documentary. I'm sure Elise will want shots of them," I said, thinking of those super slow motion close-ups of papers—usually an incriminating letter or report—that was used on news programs to provide a visual while a voiceover described the contents.

"Of course, but they are too valuable to drag around in my luggage. No, they are under lock and key."

"A safety deposit box?"

Rafe pushed away from the bin and shook a finger at me. "Oh, no. You'll get nothing else out of me."

I sighed. "You can't blame me for trying."

"No, but from now on, my lips are sealed. I'm as quiet as a grave. And I'd appreciate it if you were, too."

"Of course. We all have a stake in the documentary and want it to be a success. And what you have will make news." I shook my head. "Oh, my gosh. Think of the headlines. You better get a publicist if you don't already have one. You're going to be swamped."

"Hmm…I'll begin practicing now. No comment. Good-bye, Kate."

WE ARE in the home stretch of the day now, I thought, as I watched our Elizabeth Bennet and Mr. Darcy pause beside a fountain and kiss. The actors ran through the scene three more times before the sun dropped so low in the sky that the light changed to the point that they couldn't film anymore. If only love were that simple, endless do-overs until everything was exactly perfect…and if it wasn't perfect, then there was always editing.

The actors left to change, and the crew began to pack up their equipment. I got to work, cleaning up the area, definitely the least glamorous part of location management. The sun had dipped behind the highest tree branches and the woods were already deep in shadow by the time we finished.

I dropped into Alex's MG with a sigh. "I'm wiped." I was too tired to care whether or not the slightly strained atmosphere that I'd felt earlier between us still existed.

"Long day," Alex said. "Especially, considering it's only your second day here."

As I agreed, I felt something catch on the heel of my shoe. I reached down and picked up a black hair scrunchy from the floorboard. I held it out to Alex. "You really do have everything in here."

"Ah—right." He tucked it into a storage compartment on his door. "You sure that's not yours?"

"Nope. Not mine."

"Must have fallen out of someone's pocket when I gave them a ride. It's quite popular, this car."

"It's cute," I murmured through a yawn. "I can see why people would want to hitch a ride."

I must have nodded off because I had no memory of the short trip through the winding hedge-lined lanes back to Nether Woodsmoor. I only started and sat up straight when Alex hit the brakes. "Sorry," he said. "They've closed our street."

Police tape stretched across the only entrance to Cottage Lane.

I was closest to a uniformed constable, so I rolled down my window. "Excuse me, can we get through? We live here."

"Sorry, no. Not until the investigation is complete."

"Investigation?"

"Yes, ma'am. A fire."

"In one of the cottages?" I asked, picturing my tiny suitcase and my meager belongings going up in smoke.

"No, in a wheelie bin."

"Oh. Well, how long do you think until we can get in?"

"Couldn't say. Possibly another hour. If you're residents, you can park and walk in on the path that goes along the back gardens."

"All right. Thank you." I cranked the handle, rolling up the window—the car was an antique and didn't have anything automatic in it.

Alex put the car in reverse and backed out the way we'd arrived. "I know where we can park." He drove down the high street then took another turn. "There's a car park here." He checked before turning in. "Yes, there are some parking spaces." He whipped the little car into one of the last spaces. "It's the beginning of one of the bike trails." We got out, and he locked the car then I followed him to a sign posted at the back of the lot with a map of the area. We walked by the sign, and he gestured to the right. "It goes over to Upper Benning. Quite a good ride, actually. Very scenic." He turned to the much smaller trail on the left. "This one meets up with the path that runs behind the cottages."

"This place is like a rabbit warren with all the paths across the countryside. How do you keep them all straight?"

"You get used to it. The paths are handy shortcuts, and everyone likes a shortcut, right?"

"Yes, I suppose so."

We reached the back gardens of the first cottage. In the small openings between the cottages, we were able to see a group of people, some of them in police uniform, moving around a plastic rolling bin with smoke drifting out of it. Twilight was fading, but there was still enough light to see the activity on the lane.

We watched for a few moments. Things seemed to be wrapping up. The constable who'd spoken to us was taking down the police tape.

"Beatrice assured me this was a nice, safe area."

"It is. Usually." Alex frowned. "This vandalism streak came on suddenly. In the last few weeks."

"Has it been all over the village?"

"I believe so. It seems random, but I haven't been paying that much attention to it." He shook his head. "Hard to understand why someone would do that—willful destruction of property.

And that bin was close to the cottage. It could have set the whole thing on fire. At least, this seems to have gotten the police's attention in a big way."

"Well, a fire is more serious than throwing rocks."

"Yes, someone could have been hurt quite badly."

Alex let out a sigh. "Hopefully, they'll catch them and then we can get back to being the sleepy village where nothing happens. Are you up for dinner tonight?"

"Yes. I haven't even bought cereal yet." We resumed walking.

"How about something different? Do you like Chinese?" Alex asked.

I stopped at the gate to my cottage. "Yes. Love it."

"Okay, there's a good place across from the White Duck. Let's go there."

"Sounds great. Twenty minutes?" I asked, looking at my watch. It was seven. "I may not be able to stay awake much longer."

"Sure."

I stepped in and closed the gate, but it was rusty and didn't want to fasten. I struggled with it for a moment. What was it with the latches and locks here? Another person, a young woman in a pale green jacket with light blond hair, was moving down the lane.

I felt a little silly standing there banging the gate repeatedly, trying to get the catch to fasten, so I smiled at her. She smiled back and continued on down the lane a few paces behind Alex. The latch finally clicked into place, and I headed up the little path to the cottage, pausing for a second to scan the twining rose vines just beginning to bud that climbed up the mellow stone. Around me, the flowerbeds gave off a rich earthy scent. I couldn't quite believe how lucky I was—I was staying in an English cottage.

◈

I POPPED the last bite of my eggroll appetizer into my mouth and leaned to the side, peering out the Bamboo Garden's window, trying to see where Alex had gone. Earlier, I had showered and changed into a white camp shirt and a fresh pair of jeans because the English evenings still felt cool to me after the boiling desert heat of California. Alex had met me in front of my cottage, and we'd walked to the Chinese restaurant. I was seated at a window table that overlooked the high street, waiting for Alex to return from stepping outside to take a phone call.

The call had come in right after we ordered, and he'd been gone quite awhile. I hadn't seen the name on the caller I.D., but I wondered if the call was from Grace. Alex and I had been at dinner together another time when he had taken a call from someone named Grace. He'd quickly stepped outside that time, too.

The breeze from the opening door stirred the leaves on the bamboo plant on the table as he returned. "I'm sorry that took so long."

"It's okay," I said. "Everything all right?"

"Fine." Our food arrived, cashew chicken for me and combination fried rice for Alex. The Bamboo Garden was located directly across the street from the pub. I'd been watching a steady stream of people arrive while I waited for Alex, and now I caught sight of Rafe, leaving the library, which was at the other end of the street, his leather messenger bag slung across his chest. He walked to the pub while talking on his phone then took a seat by the window inside the pub.

I raised my eyebrows in the direction of the White Duck. "I asked Rafe about," I glanced around the busy restaurant and lowered my voice, "that thing we discussed last night. At first, he acted like he didn't understand."

Alex deftly picked up a cluster of rice with his chopsticks. "But I bet you got him to admit it."

"How did you know?"

"I've seen you in action. When you're determined to accomplish something, there's no stopping you."

"Hmm. I'm not sure that's a compliment."

Alex grinned and chewed.

"Anyway, I found out he does have them, but not here with him. He says they are in a safe place."

"And you're dying to see them."

"Of course! Aren't you? Don't you want to see," I leaned forward and whispered, "letters in Jane Austen's handwriting?"

Alex chewed and shrugged half-heartedly.

"I can't believe it. You don't care?"

He swallowed and took a sip of his drink before answering. "Sure, I'd like to see them. It would be interesting, but it's not going to change anything, is it? She'll still be a famous author. Her books will still be the same."

I fell back against my chair. "You obviously haven't spent much time in academia."

"No," he said completely without remorse. "I did two years of college in the States, but I was much more interested in snowboarding. The whole university thing seemed a waste of time to me, especially philosophy. I know that's terrible to say. Maybe it was my professor, but it all seemed like a bunch of hogwash to me. Something is here or it's not. None of that reality and shadows of reality for me. Math, English, history, science, I get that, but the rest of it? Too esoteric for me."

"Well, esoteric or not, the academic world will go nuts when the news breaks, not to mention pop culture. It will be huge, especially if it answers questions about Austen's personal life. She and her sister were close, and we only know about a few of Jane's encounters with men because they happened when she and Cassandra were apart. She wrote to her with the details, but there's so much we don't know. Austen agreed to marry a wealthy man one night then broke off the engagement the next morning. Why? And her relatives mentioned an attachment later in life that never came to be—what happened to him. Did he die? There's been movies made—feature films—speculating about her love life and relationships. If we could really know what happened…it would be…" I trailed off at a loss for words.

"Huge," Alex supplied.

"More than huge. Gigantic. If it were an earthquake, it would be a nine-point-five."

"That must be bad, right?"

I pushed my plate away. "It's a big one. You've never been in an earthquake?"

"No, am I missing much?"

"Only a moment of sheer terror and then it's over."

"Sounds like snowboarding." Alex dropped his napkin by his plate. "Fancy a walk down to the river?"

"Yes."

I dropped the subject of the letters as we made our way to the river. We leaned on the balustrade, watching the water rush by, the night air soft and only a few degrees away from chilly.

"I should get you home. You've had a long day," Alex said, but didn't move.

"Yes," I agreed with my arms firmly planted on the stone. I could feel Alex's gaze on me. I turned my head to look at him.

Close-by, a siren cut through the air, startling both of us.

CHAPTER 5

"WAS THAT A FIRE TRUCK? Heading in the direction of the cottages?" I asked. I'd caught a glimpse of it at the end of the street as it sped by.

"I believe so."

"Surely there couldn't be two fires on our street in one day?"

"No, of course not. It was probably going somewhere else. Maybe there's a fire in the woods farther up the hill."

I nodded, but we had both pushed away from the bridge and were striding along as quickly as we could. If we were in Southern California where the sun baked and dried the land to the point that any wood was a potential pile of kindling, a fire in the woods might be possible. But I had a hard time picturing the damp and soggy woods catching fire, especially after yesterday's soaking rain.

We hurried up the short street to the lane with the cottages and saw the fire truck parked halfway down the street. Smoke filled the air, and I blinked away bits of ash as we hurried forward. "Is it my cottage? I can't tell." In the darkness, and with the cottages being so similar and so close to each other, I couldn't tell which one the firefighters were moving around.

"No—the one next to yours, I think."

We reached the fire truck and stopped on the edge of the lane short of Rafe's cottage. The front window to the parlor was gone, replaced by a wall of orange flame licking up the edges and flickering at the roof shingles. Firefighters moved back and forth from their truck to the cottage, carrying axes and uncoiling hoses, while others disappeared around the side of the cottage down the narrow opening that ran between the cottages. I was surprised at the firefighters pace. They weren't lollygagging, but they certainly weren't hustling around. They were going about their business with a methodical concentration, which I supposed made sense. I guess that they had to assess the situation and coordinate their plan of attack.

I glanced back at the front window. The flames seemed to have grown, like a chest expanding with a breath. They had swollen into a convex billow that curved in an arch and spread, roiling and churning, halfway up the roof.

I felt a hand on my shoulder and looked up to see Constable Albertson's craggy face. "You'll need to back away—" he broke off, searching my face. "Oh, Ms. Sharp—isn't it?"

"Yes," I said, surprised that he remembered me.

He read my expression and tapped his head by his eyebrow. "I've got a good memory for faces. And none of us have forgotten that sad business with the poor bloke who went missing. Are you staying in this cottage?"

"No. I'm in the one next door."

"Who lives here?"

"Rafe Farraday. We saw him go into the pub. But that was a while ago." I turned toward Alex. "Did you see him leave?"

"No, but he could have left when we walked down to the river."

Constable Albertson nodded. "I'll have a word with the lad in charge to let him know. Keep back." He nodded to an area on the other side of the lane away from the fire truck and the cottages.

As we moved, running footfalls pounded up the street. It was Rafe, sprinting up the middle of the lane, his messenger bag pounding against his back. He stopped short, his gaze fastened on the flames pouring out of the window. "Oh, my God."

Constable Albertson put a hand on Rafe's shoulder. "Mr. Farraday, if you'll move over here…"

"No. No, I can't. I have to get in there." He surged forward, but ran into the wall of Constable Albertson.

"You have to stay clear of the area. For your safety."

"No. I can't. You don't understand. I have to get in there. I must—it's vital." He looked around frantically.

"Is there someone else in the house?"

"No. No, no one else." He tried to dodge around the constable again, but was again blocked.

"Pets?"

"No. It's nothing like that. But I have to—"

"No," Constable Albertson overrode him, using a volume and a tone that I hadn't heard before. Rafe blinked and focused on him for the first time. Constable Albertson turned Rafe by the shoulders and marched him across to the far side of the lane. "Now. You can either wait here, or I can take you down to the station. Which will it be?"

Rafe ran a hand over his mouth and closed his eyes briefly. "Okay, I understand."

Constable Albertson hovered, staring at him intently for a moment. Rafe put up his hands in a gesture of surrender. "I get it. I lost it back there. Sorry. I'll stay here."

"See that you do." Constable Albertson walked away, but gave Rafe several long glances over his shoulder.

I looked back to the cottage. The smell of smoke and burning wood filled the air. Several firefighters were in position around the cottage. Water coursed through the hoses, arching through the air. The front door was now open, and firefighters were moving into the house.

Rafe watched for a moment, then turned away. His peaked eyebrows stood out darkly against his pale face. He ran his hands up into his hair then bent over double. I exchanged a glance with Alex. "Do you think he's going to be sick?"

Alex put a hand on Rafe's shoulder. "You okay, buddy?"

Rafe groaned then slowly collapsed. Alex steadied him, helping him to sit down. I crouched down on his other side. "It's terrible, I know. But at least you weren't in there and," I strained to look up over the fire truck. "I don't see any flames now. I'm sure there will be damage, but it looks like they've managed to save most of the cottage."

Rivulets of water streamed across the lane and soaked into the grass where Rafe sat. He didn't notice. "It doesn't matter. It's too late. They're gone."

"What's gone?"

"The letters."

I thudded down beside him, my knees squishing into the damp grass. "The Jane Austen letters?"

He nodded, a stricken look on his face.

"But you said you didn't have them. That they were safe."

He mumbled something.

"What?"

"I lied, okay? I don't care if you've got a Pulitzer Prize in literature, I wasn't about to tell you that I had the letters with me."

"Where? Where were they?"

Rafe sighed. "In the parlor."

"In some sort of storage container, right? If it was metal..."

"No. I kept them in an archival box. Acid-free, of course," he said, his tone edged with giddiness.

Alex murmured my name in a warning tone. I pulled my gaze away from Rafe.

"He's in shock. Go easy on him," Alex mouthed, then looked pointedly at the tight grip I had on Rafe's arm.

I released his arm and sent Alex a frustrated look. "You don't understand the significance of those letters."

"They are *pieces of paper*," Alex said. "We're not talking about the Magna Carta, but even then, its not like anything is as valuable as a human life. Rafe, you had a lucky escape tonight."

"Were," Rafe said miserably. "They *were* pieces of paper. There's no way they survived." He pointed at the cottage, which now had black, sooty streaks on the stone around the gaping hole where the front window had been.

I sent Alex a sour look. "I understand those papers weren't as valuable as a person, but they were important."

"To literary geeks."

I frowned at him, but before I could say anything else, Constable Albertson joined us.

Rafe asked, "When can I get back inside?"

"Not for a while. A few days, I suspect."

"But surely I can go in now, see the extent of the damage."

"No, it's a crime scene."

Rafe swallowed. "It was arson?"

I'd been staring across the street, watching the firefighters. They were still moving around the cottage as well as in and out of the front door, but there was something about Rafe's tone that drew my attention back to him. He sounded—what? Frightened and...anxious, maybe? I couldn't quite decide.

Constable Albertson ignored Rafe's question. "Mr. Farraday, you stated that no one else was in the cottage."

"Yes, that's right."

"So to your knowledge, your cottage was empty?"

"Yes."

Constable Albertson sighed. "They've found a body."

CHAPTER 6

THE NEXT MORNING, I SHOULDERED my tote bag, slipped my phone in my pocket, then stepped outside and managed to lock my front door on my second try—I was getting better—before turning to survey the scene. Rafe's cottage and front garden were decimated. Plants and grass were trampled into a muddy mess, and a pile of charred wooden debris sat near the lane. In the sunlight, the black smoke stains looked even darker and more ominous than they had in the pulsing lights of the emergency vehicles last night.

Two men in coveralls were preparing to place a board over the gap where the window had been. The small section of the interior of the cottage that I could see didn't look anything like a home. It was a charred conglomeration of shapes. Police tape ringed the yard, wrapping alongside the yews all the way to the back garden.

I was surprised I'd been allowed to return to my cottage last night, but after waiting several hours, Constable Albertson had told Alex and me that residents were allowed to return to their homes. The fire had been contained within the front room and the interior hallway of Rafe's cottage. It was completely out, and there was no danger of it reigniting.

I hadn't slept well. At Rafe's cottage, a constant flow of activity—the investigation team I imagined—continued until the early hours of the morning.

"Looks horrible, doesn't it?" a voice called behind me, and I turned. Beatrice had parked her rusty Land Rover at the edge of the police tape and now walked up the path to stand beside me. "Well, at least the walls are still intact," she said, hands on her hips as she looked over the cottage. "It's a good thing Jenny Templeton smelled the fire when she took her dog out for its nightly walk; otherwise, the whole lot could have gone up."

I shivered. The fire I'd seen had been a powerful, hungry thing. I didn't want to think about how awful it would have been if all the cottages had caught fire.

I spotted Alex walking down the street, his backpack slung over his shoulder. He'd shaved this morning, but his hair was still its usual tousled style, and his white shirt was crinkled. He detoured around the police tape and joined us. We exchanged good mornings, but all of our attention was on the burnt cottage.

"Pretty grim sight in the light of day," Alex said.

"So do they know what happened? How it started?" I asked.

Beatrice shook her head. "No. Or, if they do they're keeping it to themselves. All they've told me is that the body was a woman."

A car in low gear moved up the street and parked behind the Land Rover. Detective Chief Inspector Quimby emerged from the car and strode across the grass to us, his attention fixed on Beatrice. "Lady Stone, thank you for meeting me here."

"Of course. You remember Alex Norcutt and Kate Sharp."

Quimby gave us all quick nods of acknowledgement. "Yes. Back for another visit, Ms. Sharp?" The first time I'd met Quimby he'd been dressed head-to-toe in brown, which along with his brown hair, had given him a plain, fade-away look until I noticed his sharp green eyes. Today he was again in a brown suit, but he was branching out. A stripe of navy ran through his tie.

"No, I'm working," I replied, "with Alex on the Jane Austen documentary."

He looked sharply toward Alex, his eyebrows raised. "Another film?"

He didn't sound happy about it, and I couldn't blame him. The last film project had complicated his work life quite a bit.

"Yes," Alex said.

"Planning to film in and around Nether Woodsmoor, I suppose?"

"Already filming," Alex said.

"So what can you tell us about this poor woman who was found last night, DCI Quimby?" Beatrice asked.

"Not much yet. She was young, mid-twenties, no identification on her. I'm in charge of the response unit, which was set up last evening in the church hall. No reports of a missing woman in the area, so we are making inquiries farther afield."

"Have you been able to determine what happened?" Beatrice pressed.

"You mean whether or not it was murder?" Quimby asked. "I'm afraid so. She was hit on the back of the head rather viciously. The medical examiner has determined the injury occurred before the injuries from the fire."

Beatrice said, "Worse and worse. It's horrible that she died, awful, but to know that it was intentional...that makes it so much more disturbing."

"Quite," Quimby murmured, his gaze ranging over the blackened stones.

Beatrice continued, "Horrible for the poor young woman, and such a shame for us as well. We've worked so hard to make Nether Woodsmoor known as a peaceful country getaway."

Quimby sighed. "Yes. There's significant pressure to find the culprit quickly." He turned to look at Honeysuckle Cottage. "Who lives here?"

"I do," I said. "Only for the last two days, though, so I'm afraid I won't be much help to you."

"You knew Mr. Farraday?"

"Yes, I scouted his cottage as a location to film his interview."

"He's involved in the film project, too?" He pulled his cell phone from his pocket and flicked through the screens. "He gave his occupation last night as a lecturer. A literature professor, I believe he called himself."

"Yes, he is, but he's providing commentary for the documentary."

Quimby asked, "Is there anyone in this village not associated with the filming?"

"I doubt it," Beatrice said, "between lodging, feeding, and outfitting the cast and crew, the whole town has probably either met someone involved in the production, if not sold them something."

Quimby didn't look happy. He refocused on me. "So, in the short time you knew him, did you notice a woman around Mr. Farraday's cottage?"

"No."

"Did he mention a woman when you did your... scouting...bit?"

"No, we didn't talk much, only about the local vandalism and about books."

"I see," Quimby said as if that was strange. Beside him, Alex had the same look on his face.

"Mr. Norcutt, you've lived here much longer. Did you ever see a woman with Mr. Farraday?"

"Yes, Becca Ford is his particular friend."

Quimby tapped the information into his phone then said to Beatrice, "If you have a few moments, I'd like you to walk through the cottage with me."

"Yes, I figured as much. I brought my Wellies." She moved back to her car and removed a pair of galoshes.

Alex and I had been dismissed, so I led the way down the lane as Alex asked, "Did you get the text?"

"No." I pulled out my phone to double check, but I had no new messages or missed calls.

"Elise has called an emergency meeting at the inn. Want to ride with me?"

I put my phone away with a sigh. "Yes. Speaking of that, we need to talk about my transportation issue. What about these cars that you mentioned? The ones the production rented."

"Yeah, about that." Alex cleared his throat. "I mentioned it to Elise yesterday. She said since you're staying so close to me, we can carpool." We reached the MG, and Alex opened the passenger door for me. "Sorry."

"So, I don't get use of the rental cars, and she won't even add me to her contact list so that I know what's going on?"

"Let me send a text to Mary about the notifications," Alex said as he tapped on his phone. "She'll get you on there. About the car, well, Elise said something about insurance and driver's license issues."

"I have my International Driver's Permit. I'm perfectly legal to drive in the U.K."

"Yeah, I thought that was bunk, but I couldn't talk her out of it. Maybe you can."

"No, I'm going to keep my head down and get my work done." I moved a plastic bag and several pieces of junk mail out of the passenger seat. Alex nodded and closed my door. "And walk," I said to myself as Alex moved around the car. "Looks like I'm going to be doing a lot of walking."

～

MY PLAN TO keep my head down didn't exactly work out. The moment we joined the group at the long table in the inn's restaurant, Elise skewered me with an angry look. "What's this about a fire in Rafe Farraday's cottage?" she asked as if I was personally responsible for the situation. She was dressed in black again today, a high ribbed turtleneck and black jeans. The dark color only accented the paleness of her face and the dark circles under her eyes.

I swallowed the defensive reply that came to my lips and instead gave her a quick summary of what had happened.

"So there's no way to use the location?" she asked.

"No, the fire totally destroyed the front room, and the whole cottage is a crime scene because of the body they found."

Melissa stopped stirring her tea, Felix looked up from his phone, and Paul's pen hovered over his clipboard.

"I thought you would have heard," I said.

"That news hadn't traveled as far as Upper Benning," Elise said. "Do they know who it was?"

"No, they haven't been able to identify the body. A young woman in her twenties is all they know now."

"Accident or murder?"

"Murder," I said.

"And Mr. Farraday is embroiled in this?" Elise said, her tone tinged with distaste.

"I don't know. He was stunned when the police told him about the body." I looked toward Alex, who nodded his agreement as he passed me a cup of coffee.

I took a long sip. I still wasn't fully adjusted to the time change, and getting up this morning had felt like I was dragging myself out of bed in the middle of the night. As Alex raised his coffee cup to his lips, he murmured the word, "Letters?" so low that only I could hear him.

I gave a warning shake of my head. There was no way I was breaking the news to Elise that the Jane Austen letters had gone up in the fire. That was something that Rafe could tell her himself.

Alex sent me a half smile before drinking from his cup. He understood.

Elise's voice snapped my attention back to her. "We need another location. I suppose we could use the library at Parkview Hall." She tapped her pen on the table.

"The library is off limits to filming," Alex said.

"What?" Elise said.

"It's in the contract. Sir Harold was worried about the damage the lights could do to the books. It was one of the tradeoffs we made to get Parkview Hall."

Elise wrinkled her lips to one side. "Yes, I remember that bit," she said reluctantly. "Seemed a good thing at the time. Well, I suppose we could run him up to London and interview him with the other experts next week."

"Not if he's a murder suspect," Felix said.

Elise pinned her gaze on Felix. "He's a suspect?"

Felix didn't seem the least bit uncomfortable under her scrutiny. "Dead body found in his burnt-out cottage? The police may not want him scampering off to London...or anywhere else, for that matter."

Elise frowned. "That's true. If he did have something to do with it, we need to find out. A large portion of the hook for this documentary depends on Rafe Farraday and his material." Elise swiveled her focus to me. "Find out if he's involved, and get us a new location, somewhere nearby with lots of books in the background for his interview. We'll carry on as if everything is fine unless you find something that indicates he's going to be implicated in the murder. If that's the case, we'll have to drop him." Elise picked up a piece of paper. "Which would be a shame because he comes across so well on camera, but if he's a murderer, well, it can't be helped, I suppose. Better to cut ties now than have the whole project tainted. All right, moving on to today's schedule. We start at noon to catch the best light in the drawing room windows at Parkview Hall—"

I cut in quickly, "But you'd need a private detective for something like that. There's no way that I can—"

Elise slapped the paper down. "Our budget doesn't include private detectives, and you apparently have a knack for that sort of…" she circled her hand in the air "…thing. It seems you're the perfect person for it. Oh yes, we've all heard about what happened last time you were in Nether Woodsmoor. You're quite the little celebrity here. I suggest you get to it immediately. Alex can handle the shoot this afternoon. Find out what you can about Rafe Farraday and send a scouting report for possible new interview locations."

I sat a moment, feeling a bit like Alice talking to the Queen of Hearts.

Elise had picked up her paper again. When I didn't move, she tilted her head, inquiringly. "Problem?"

She was looking for an excuse to fire me. I needed this job. I had nothing lined up back in California, job-wise. And no place to live. My lease had expired this month. Since I had planned to move to a new apartment anyway, I'd given up my apartment and put most of my things in storage in California.

A return to the States would mean moving in with my mother, at least temporarily. I loved my mom, but I didn't want to go back to fighting off her constant attempts to fix me up with eligible men. Anyone who was male and had a pulse qualified for that category in my mother's opinion.

And, I really wanted to stay in England for a while.

The misgivings I'd felt when I first arrived had faded. I liked my snug cottage and the unrelenting green landscape, which was so different from the dusty gray-brown hills of Southern California. I liked listening to the cadence of the British accent in all its varieties. I liked the quieter more rural lifestyle in Nether Woodsmoor, well, except for the vandalism and the murder, but those things weren't the norm. They were aberrations. I hadn't even had a chance to explore the trails and paths on my own. I loved hiking and wanted to get out and have a good "ramble," as the Brits called it, among the hills and valleys around the village.

"No. No problem at all." I stood and settled my tote bag on my shoulder. "I'll get back to you as soon as I know something."

I strode away, head held high, and got to the inn's door before I realized I was going to have to spoil my exit by crawling back and asking for a car. I turned and found Alex a few strides behind me. "Take my car." He handed me his keys. "I can catch a ride with someone here out to Parkview Hall. We'll go directly there in a little while to get started with set-up."

"Oh, I don't know."

"You have your International Driver's Permit. You're fully qualified to drive in the U.K."

He grinned at me as he echoed my words from earlier today, and I couldn't help but smile back. "That is true. I'll be careful."

"Oh, and you might check Grove Cottage. I'm pretty sure that's where Rafe went last night after the fire. When I left, he was calling Becca, asking if she could come pick him up."

"Thanks," I said. "Sounds like a good place to start."

Despite having an International Driver's Permit, I was a bit rusty in the area of driving a car with a standard transmission. I was glad the inn's parking lot was deserted as I lurched into gear and merged onto the road that would take me to Becca's cottage. I remembered the way from my last visit to Nether Woodsmoor. It wasn't far, but by the time I neared Grove Cottage, a fine sheen of sweat covered my face. I had to fight my instinct to drive on the right. At every roundabout I gripped the steering wheel and chatted the mantra I'd used when I drove the last time I was in England, *stay left, stay left.*

I saw the gates to Grove Cottage and breathed a sigh of relief. They were open, thank goodness, which meant I wouldn't have to do that tricky half gas pedal, half clutch maneuver to keep the car from rolling back down the hill while I spoke into an intercom. I hit the gas and accelerated up the hill to the gates with a burst of speed. My seat suddenly slid back, slamming into the position farthest away from the steering wheel, jerking my hands off the wheel and leaving my toes just brushing the pedals. I flailed there for a moment, trying to inch my way forward. The little MG sailed through the gates, crested the hill, and began the immediate descent down a steep slope that allowed me to scoot forward to the edge of the seat and get my hands firmly on the wheel as I applied the brake, coming to a stop on the gravel sweep beside a dark sedan near the front door of the two-story yellow house.

I put on the parking brake and took a moment to let my heartbeat calm down. Once I wasn't breathing like I'd just run sprints, I adjusted the seat, pulling it back into position, then pressed my feet against the floorboard, trying to push it back. It held for a moment then flew back to the far position again. Alex had long legs. I'd had to adjust the seat forward when I got in the car. I bet he always drove with the seat in the setting the farthest away from the steering wheel. He might not even be aware that the seat didn't completely lock out in the other slot. I gingerly returned it to the position closer to the steering wheel and got out of the car.

Located in a valley and backed by a woodland, Grove Cottage had been on the list of potential locations for the *Pride and Prejudice* film. "Cottage" was a misnomer for the building. I followed the maid who had opened the door through the entry, which was larger than all of Honeysuckle Cottage, and around a large table with a vase of flowers so tall and extravagant that the center blooms almost touched the chandelier suspended above them.

The house was quiet, and the maid's heels clicked loudly along the hardwood floors until we reached the plush rug covering the floor of a sitting room, which was decorated in pale yellow, cream, and pastel green. I took a seat on a Queen Anne wingback chair upholstered in a green and cream lattice pattern. I sat with my knees swiveled to one side, my feet together, and my hands in my lap. It was the sort of room that made you feel like you had to be on your best behavior.

Books and framed photos were spread across gleaming hardwood tables in seemingly casual arrangements, but every pillow was plumped to maximum fullness, and there wasn't a speck of dust anywhere. It looked so perfect that I felt as if I had walked into a *Country Home* article.

The day was beautiful, and the windows were open to the cool morning air. The sound of voices drifted in through the windows. I'd taken out my phone to check my messages, but then a voice spoke, and my head came up. I'd heard that voice earlier this morning.

I moved to the open window and saw Quimby's suited figure seated in a wicker chair on a flagstone terrace at the side of the house, his back to the windows. Across from him, Rafe and Becca sat on a matching sofa. Becca tilted her red-gold head to listen to the murmur from the maid. Even this far away, I could tell that Becca was less than pleased to hear my name. She sighed impatiently and waved the maid away, then turned back to Quimby. Apparently, I was a guest who could be kept waiting.

I moved to the window closest to them and could hear Quimby saying, "...when did you last open the cupboard under the stairs?"

Rafe shrugged one shoulder. "I don't know. Weeks ago probably. What has that got to do with anything?" He had one arm flung along the back of the sofa behind Becca's shoulders. His other elbow rested on the arm of the sofa. His shoulders tilted in the direction of his bent arm as he propped his head against his hand. He looked tired, but not especially worried. Had Quimby not told him the woman who died in his cottage had been murdered?

"It's where the body was found."

Becca huffed and inched closer to Rafe. "I can't believe you're asking these types of questions. Of course, Rafe doesn't know a thing about this...person."

"Woman," Quimby corrected. "A young woman, mid-twenties, about five-feet-three inches tall. One-hundred-sixty centimeters."

Becca's face settled into sulky lines. "See? Far too young for Rafe."

"Perhaps one of your students?" Quimby asked.

"No. I haven't seen anyone I know from the United States here. I'm on sabbatical, after all. Getting away from my normal routines, you know."

"So you haven't been visited or contacted by a student recently?"

I blew out a long breath. It seemed that Felix was right, that Quimby was seriously considering Rafe as a possible suspect.

"No."

Quimby handed a piece of paper to Rafe. "Do you recognize this woman?"

Rafe frowned at the paper. "No. I'm sorry."

Becca looked it over, a sour expression on her face. "Tolerable, but nothing special. I doubt if I'd remember her if I had seen her. But, in any case, no, that person doesn't look familiar to me either."

"Where were you yesterday afternoon and evening?"

Rafe lifted his head away from his hand, and his relaxed posture disappeared. "What is this? It was some sort of bizarre accident, wasn't it?"

"We're assessing the whereabouts of everyone in the neighborhood yesterday."

"It was murder, then. And you think I did it," he said in a tone of wonderment.

"This is absurd," Becca sputtered. She reached for her cell phone, which was on a wicker table beside the sofa. "Don't say another word. I'll call my solicitor."

Rafe put a hand on her arm, but didn't look at her. He fixed his attention on Quimby. "No need. I worked in the library all afternoon, until they closed at eight, in fact. They had to kick me out. I went from there to the pub. I'm sure several people there will remember me," he said.

"And you stayed inside the pub how long?"

"Until a group of people came in babbling about a fire in Cottage Lane. After what happened with the wheelie bin, I figured I should check it out." His conceited tone faded. "I didn't expect to see flames halfway up the roof when I arrived. It was shocking. I—well, I lost it for a moment. The local bobbie had to hold me back. I expect you already know about that bit."

Becca put her phone down slowly. "You didn't tell me that."

"My research," he said with a quick grimace. "I wasn't thinking straight. I wanted to go in and get it, but obviously it was gone. As I said, not thinking straight." Rafe removed his arm from the back of the sofa and leaned forward. "Have you figured out how it started?"

"Our investigators found shattered glass on the floor and a rock in the room, which appears to have hit a lamp and over-turned it. The light was on, and heat from the bulb caught the shade on fire, which then ignited the rug. Once the rug caught fire, it spread quickly throughout the room."

"So it was vandalism," Becca said, straightening her shoulders, seemingly glad to move back to outrage, which seemed to be her forte. "Really, this is disgraceful. The police should have put a stop to it long ago. A few more patrols would have taken care of it, I'm sure."

"The Nether Woodsmoor constabulary is stretched thin

already, Mrs. Ford. They don't have the manpower to patrol every street all night long."

"Then they should increase the number of officers. If things are let go, this is what happens."

"Murder?" Quimby asked.

"No, of course not. What happened with that person, I mean, woman," she said after Quimby sent her a sharp look, "had to be a horrible accident. You said yourself that you're only checking everyone's whereabouts."

"The woman *was* murdered. She was struck on the back of the head prior to the fire."

"Well, she must have fallen while she was in the cottage and knocked herself out. Then the smoke…"

"I can assure you that the wounds, the type and severity, were not caused by a fall."

Instead of acknowledging that she was in the wrong, Becca simply changed tacks. "Well, I'm sure more details will emerge. She must have been…" She flicked her fingers. "Part of a group of vagrants who happened to pick Rafe's cottage to break into. One murdered the other one during the robbery or something like that."

"Purely coincidence that Mr. Farraday's cottage was involved?" Quimby asked, disbelief heavy in his tone.

"What else could it be?"

"Many other things," Quimby said repressively, but Becca was on a roll.

"I'm sure it was one of those…what do they call them on the telly? Crimes of opportunity," She bobbed her head in an assured nod. "Someone saw Rafe leave. It's no secret he has a nice laptop. He carries it around the village constantly. That's probably what she was after."

"If he carries it around the village, wouldn't it most likely have been with him? And how did she get in the cottage? The locks were not tampered with. Fire services had to cut the door and locks to get inside. Do you think your random thieving woman was also an expert lock pick?"

"Oh, it's no problem to get into the cottages on that lane." Becca waved a hand and sat back, a patronizing smile on her face. "Everyone knows the keys to the cottages are practically interchangeable, and a screwdriver works just as well in a pinch. Our maid lived in one of the cottages for a short time. Told us all about it."

"So you're saying the locks *aren't* secure?" Quimby asked sharply.

"I'm afraid so," Rafe said. "That's why Beatrice had the slider bolts. The night latches are decrepit. Not hard to jimmy at all."

"And the bolts on your doors, did you use them?"

"Not the front door, no, because that's the way I left for the pub. And the back door," Rafe stared at the house, and I faded to the left a bit. I was standing well inside the window casing, so he shouldn't have been able to see me, but I didn't want to be caught eavesdropping. Rafe looked back to Quimby. "No, I don't think so. Hard to say for sure, but I doubt it."

Rafe looked toward the windows again, so I moved back to the chair, thinking about when I'd held the square of wood in place so Rafe could repair his door. I was almost sure the bolt had been locked into place so that the door couldn't be opened, but I supposed he could have opened it sometime between when I'd seen it and last evening.

CHAPTER 7

"SO YOU DIDN'T TELL ELISE about the letters?" Rafe asked. "Why not?"

I put down the cup of tea that Becca had reluctantly told the maid to fetch before excusing herself from the room. "Because I'm not that brave," I said.

Rafe's face broke into a grin. "She's quite...um...focused, shall we say?"

"Yes, let's leave it at that. And I'm already in her bad books."

"Why?"

"I wish I knew." I leaned back in the chair I'd occupied earlier. Despite looking very pretty, it wasn't comfortable. "When will you tell her?"

I knew I really should ask him about the murder. That's what Elise wanted me to do. Quiz him on his involvement. No, quiz was too mild a word to use in association with Elise. An inquisition seemed more Elise's style. Quimby's questions indicated he was interested in Rafe's movements, but Rafe said he was in the library all afternoon. I knew Elise would want a verbal confirmation of his whereabouts. I didn't think she'd hang the continuation of the production on an overheard conversation, but so far I hadn't figured out a way to work the conversation around to the murder. I'm not normally shy about getting to the point, but it seemed like a smarter move to tread carefully.

Rafe lounged in another of the Queen Anne chairs, his leg slung over the arm, a cup of tea cradled at his midsection. "It will have to be soon. I'm supposed to produce the letters for filming." He frowned at the ceiling. "I still can't believe I was so foolish. I should have kept the letters in a safety deposit box as you suggested."

"But you have copies."

"Of course I had copies." Rafe licked his lips. "But they were with the originals."

"What?"

"I know. I know." Rafe sat up suddenly and pushed his teacup onto the tray roughly, causing a clatter of china. He paced to the windows then back. "I didn't want to handle the originals. To prevent further damage and deterioration, you know. So I was working from the copies. It was easier to keep them all together. The copies were on top; the originals at the bottom. I should have separated them." He paced back to the window.

"Well, then during the authentication process...photographs would have been taken or copies or scans or something, right?"

Rafe didn't reply right away, continuing to stare out the window.

"I was told that you'd had them authenticated..." I said.

"I did, but I've become a victim of my own paranoia. I was so worried about being scooped, of word leaking out about what I'd found, that I went to an extremely discreet lab in what I jokingly called an undisclosed location, and required everyone involved to sign various agreements. One of those agreements was a nondis-closure agreement."

He didn't go on, only stared out the window. "And?" I prompted.

He sighed. "The other agreements required the lab to destroy all files and records of their procedures."

"What?"

"I only have the analysis of the lab that the paper and ink are consistent with what was used during Jane Austen's time and the handwriting analysis report."

I tried to speak, but my amazement strangled the words in my throat. I carefully set down my teacup and cleared my throat. "Of all the sloppy, unprofessional things—"

He turned back to me, speaking quickly. "You know what the world is like now. A text, a mention on any social media, and I'd be blown. I *had* to be careful. The exclusivity was what would make the book."

"And your career," I said. He'd made a decision on what was best for him, angling to get all the mileage out of his find that he could. "You could have released the letters as soon as you had the authentication. They're lost forever now."

"I know." He massaged his forehead. "You don't know how many times I've gone over it in my mind. I couldn't sleep last night, thinking if only I'd done this or that. But would you? I mean, think about it." He moved back to the chair near me and sat down. He propped his elbows on his knees and leaned over the tea tray. "If you'd found them, can you really tell me you would have magnanimously released the letters without at least trying to gain something from it, personally?"

I looked away. "No, you're right." I would have thought about how I could leverage the letters as well, maybe as an entrance back into a grad program or simply as a way to become an expert with a book or two to my name. "But you have to have notes, right?" I asked. "Even snippets of Austen's letters would be better than nothing."

"Yes." He nodded slowly.

"And you can remember the gist of some of them?"

"Of course. I've spent hours reading and rereading them."

"Well, it sounds like you need to get what you remember down on paper. And make some copies. Back it up."

"Yes." He'd stood again and paced around the room, mumbling to himself, his focus turned inward.

Before I lost him completely, I said, "Rafe, we need a new place to shoot the interview."

"What?" He looked at me, but his thoughts were far away.

"The interview. We need a new location to film it. Perhaps here? Is there a study or library? Elise liked the look we had in your cottage with lots of books in the background."

"Sure. Come with me."

Rafe left the tea things and trotted up the stairs then opened a door to a room with a desk and several club chairs. Several glass-fronted bookcases filled the walls. "I was trying to get some work done this morning before the DCI arrived."

"This might do," I said, glancing around the room. I pushed back the heavy velvet drapes and bright sunlight flooded in, glinting off the glass. It would be tricky, getting the light right and avoiding glaring reflection, but I thought we could make it work—as long as Elise didn't cut Rafe from the documentary.

Rafe moved to the desk where a laptop sat beside a messenger bag. He sat down and placed his hands on the keys.

"Your laptop escaped the fire?"

"Yes, I had it with me." He patted the messenger bag. "Fortunate, that. I would be lost without it."

"Hmm. And too bad for any would-be thief," I said, "if you buy Becca's theory."

Rafe didn't reply, so I took out my camera, photographed the room, and made notes. "Do you think Becca will mind if we interview here?" I asked as I moved from one corner to the other.

"Are you kidding?" He glanced quickly at the door and lowered his voice. "Anything to get close to notoriety."

I raised my eyebrows, but Rafe already had his head bent over his laptop again.

Unlike the last time I had out my camera around Rafe, he hardly looked up. I finished, packed my things away, and said we'd be in touch about the interview. "Sure. Good," he said as he typed away.

I'd found a possible location for the interview, but as far as Rafe's guilt or innocence...well, I hadn't been able to subtly work it into the conversation, and I couldn't go back to Elise with information I'd learned through eavesdropping. I might as well try the direct approach. "Rafe, did you have anything to do with that woman's death? I'm sorry to ask, but it's critical that the production have all the information..."

"Hmm?" The movement of his fingers slowed.

"The woman found in your cottage. Were you...involved...in her death in any way?"

"No, of course not," he said matter-of-factly as his fingers resumed their quick tapping. "No idea how she came to be there."

"Okay. We'll be in touch."

I went down the stairs slowly, surprised to realize that I believed him. There was something so calm and straightforward in his manner. There was no sign of the smugness he'd shown earlier with Quimby. He didn't seem to be lying, but then again, detecting when someone was lying was not something I had a lot of experience with. I wondered what Quimby would think if he'd been there.

Becca was waiting for me at the bottom of the stairs, her arms crossed. "Rafe showed you the study?" she asked, her carefully plucked eyebrows arching. Or at least, it appeared she was trying to raise her eyebrows, but her incredibly smooth forehead didn't want to give a centimeter. She'd changed into riding breeches, which skimmed her slim figure, and had woven her red-gold hair into a braid that fell across one shoulder.

"Yes. The production planned to interview Rafe in his cottage, but now we need to make alternate arrangements. Rafe thought the study might work," I said, not sure how she would react. The interactions we'd had during the pre-production for the feature film hadn't gone well, to put it mildly.

She uncrossed her arms. "How much?" she asked crisply, and I knew she was in.

"I'll discuss it with the producer and get back to you this afternoon."

"Good." She opened the door. "Have Alex call me. He and I worked so closely together last time. He knows exactly what I want." She managed to make the words into a *double entendre*.

I knew that if we used Grove House, Alex would want to stay as far away from Becca as possible, but I managed to keep a straight face as I said, "I'll pass along your request."

"See that you do." Becca closed the door the moment I crossed the threshold. I was lucky I didn't get my heel caught in the door. I shook my head and braced myself to drive back to the village.

I ROLLED to a stop in front of my cottage and took a moment to do some deep breathing. I'd had to repeat the slipping back, struggling forward procedure on the way out of Becca's drive, but I'd been ready for it this time and had managed to struggle forward once the car was on level ground and readjust the seat. Fortunately, the road back to Nether Woodsmoor didn't have any sharp inclines, but I had made a wrong turn which took me into the center of Nether Woodsmoor, which wasn't difficult to navigate or congested by any means—it certainly wasn't London or Manchester—but by the time I turned onto Cottage Lane, my palms were sweaty, and I was as jittery as a thoroughbred before a race. I'd returned to Honeysuckle Cottage so I could download my photos and put all the information together for Elise on a possible new interview location.

I'd made a stop on the way back to the cottage, the local library. I wanted to give Elise several options so she couldn't complain, but while the library was located in a picturesque golden stone building with hanging flower baskets outside the front door, the inside had been totally remodeled. The gray metal bookshelves with their industrial look did not convey the "country estate library" vibe that Elise wanted.

While I was inside the library, I asked the woman at the checkout counter if she'd worked yesterday, hoping she could tell me if Rafe had been in the library all afternoon, but she shook her head. "That'd be Christina. She's usually here, but had an appointment today. Do you need a library card? I'm afraid only she can do that. I'm only a volunteer."

I told her it was fine, that I'd drop in again later, and then I returned to the MG. Before I got on the road again, I had found Beatrice's phone number on the list of contact info Alex had sent me. I left a message on Beatrice's voicemail, asking if she knew of any other locations in homes or other buildings around the area that had a study or library that might work for the interview. Becca might be on-board with the idea of the interview taking place at her house, but we didn't have anything in writing yet, and I always like to have a backup plan, especially when the home owner was as mercurial as Becca.

I stepped out of the car and surveyed Lilac Cottage as I walked to my door. The crime tape was gone, and a crew of men in coveralls and heavy gloves were carrying chunks of scorched wood and burnt-out furniture out of the cottage and heaving them into a metal dumpster, which was located directly in front of Rafe's cottage. I saw Quimby across the lane on his phone, his back turned away from the scene.

Half an hour later, I was putting the finishing touches on my report when a knock sounded at the front door. I had set up my laptop and spread out my notes on the round table in the kitchen.

Quimby was on the front step.

"Hello Ms. Sharp," he said, leaning so that he could see over my shoulder into the cottage. His face lit up. "Your cottage has the same layout as Mr. Farraday's cottage, yes?" I nodded. "Brilliant. Would you mind if I had a look around?"

Quimby was already lifting his foot to move across the threshold. I closed the door a bit more and stepped into the narrow gap blocking his way.

"Why?" When I met Quimby during the earlier investigation, he had been quick to suspect I was involved in that murder. I wasn't about to give him *carte blanche*. "Am I a suspect?"

"Should you be?"

"No, but you told me once that you consider everyone a suspect."

Quimby grinned. "True, but I'm not trying to gain access to your residence to search it. I simply want to see the layout of Mr. Farraday's home before the fire. And I do have a few follow-up questions to ask you. You are perfectly within your rights to deny me access. I can ask you those questions right here, if you'd rather."

"But then you might *think* I have something to hide, which I don't." I opened the door and stepped back.

"Thank you." He paused at the front room, his attention fixed on the contemporary furniture. "Ah…interesting."

"Isn't it?" I let him hang for an awkward moment then said, "It belonged to the former tenant."

"Ah." He walked around the room, examined the window, then eyed the space between the window and my couch. He moved back into the hall, looked up the stairs, but didn't go up, then touched the door to the storage space under the stairs. "May I?"

"Go ahead." I waved a hand, but then felt a frisson of doubt. There hadn't been anything unusual or…incriminating…in there when I put my suitcase away, had there? I hadn't really looked around. I'd just shoved it in and closed the door.

Quimby switched on a pencil-sized flashlight. I stepped closer and watched over his shoulder as the bright circle illuminated my small suitcase then a mop, broom, and tank vacuum. I tried to keep my sigh of relief inaudible. Quimby moved my suitcase slightly, then hunched over and entered the small space. "Not expansive, but room enough for a body even with more items than you have stored in here."

"I suppose so," I said, trying not to think about how horrible it would be to be trapped in a burning house.

Quimby closed the door and looked toward the kitchen. "May I?"

"Yes, of course," I said, still thinking about the unknown woman.

I followed Quimby into the kitchen. He examined the back-door then retraced his steps through the kitchen to the hallway. He walked the route several times, then said, "Would you mind if I tried an experiment on the lock on your backdoor? I've cleared it with Lady Stone."

"Are you going to try and open it without a key?"

He blinked, and before he could assume that I had been eaves-dropping on his earlier conversation—something that I was sure he would frown on—I said, "Beatrice told me the locks on these cottages are not very secure. That's why the bolt is there."

"Right. Unfortunately, the fire service had to damage the locks on the doors of Mr. Farraday's cottage to get inside. They're not in good shape."

"Yes, sure. Give it a go. I've had so much trouble getting the locks to open that I've certainly wished I had another way to get inside."

Quimby gave a small smile then stepped onto the back porch. I swiped up the set of keys that I'd left on the kitchen table and hurried outside after him. I managed to lock the door from the outside with the key after two attempts, then stepped back.

Quimby examined the lock with his slim flashlight then removed a screwdriver from a pocket of his jacket. After about three experimental twists of varying pressure, the lock clicked and the door swung open easily.

"Well, that's frightening," I said, mentally vowing to always use the bolt lock. "Do you think the front lock would be as easy to open?"

"I assume so. They are the same model of lock, but I'd like to try it."

We trooped to the front door, our heels tapping loudly on the hardwood floor. We repeated the process, but this time, it took Quimby only one attempt to get the door open. I glanced at him out of the corner of my eye. "You're awfully good at this breaking and entering stuff."

"I'm a quick study, Ms. Sharp," he said blandly as he removed a package of tissues from his pocket and wiped down the screwdriver before putting it away. "Thank you. That was very helpful."

"Sure. You can attempt to break into my place anytime, just give me a heads up so you don't scare me to death."

The trace of humor on his face vanished. "This is a one-time event. An experiment. I'd never authorize anyone to try something like this without the resident's permission."

"It's okay. I was joking. Well, partly. I do intend to keep the bolts locked whenever I'm home."

"That would be wise. Now, just a few more questions, if you have the time?"

The workers next door were giving us curious glances, and I noticed a woman who lived in the cottage at the end of the lane was taking an extra-long time to make her way up the path to her cottage as she squinted in our direction. "Yes, let's go back inside."

I started to offer him a seat on the couch, then said, "The kitchen will be more comfortable, I think," and led the way down the hallway. "I'd offer you a cup of tea, but I'm afraid I haven't even been to the store yet to buy food. I could get you a glass of water, though."

"No need. This will only take a moment." Quimby pulled out a chair at the kitchen table, and I sat down opposite him. "Have you thought of anything that might be helpful to our investigation?"

"Um, no." My thoughts veered to the letters, but they had nothing to do with the woman. Unless she was in the cottage looking for them? In the cupboard under the stairs? No.

Perhaps Rafe put her there, a contrary voice whispered, but Quimby was already asking his next question.

"What time did you leave your cottage last night?"

"It was seven-twenty or a little after."

"You remember the exact time?"

"Yes. When Alex and I parted at the back gate we made plans to go to dinner in twenty minutes. It was seven then."

"I'm sorry, what's this about the back gate?"

I explained about the lane being blocked earlier that evening because of the fire in the bin, and how we had to park in the lot for the bike trail. "So we walked home along the path behind the cottages," I said.

He flicked to another screen on his phone. "After that, you went to the Chinese restaurant across the street from the pub? How did you get there?"

"We walked."

"And how long were you at dinner?"

I shrugged. "I don't know, maybe forty-five minutes, maybe an hour."

"And at some point, you saw Mr. Farraday arrive at the pub. What time was that?"

"I'm not sure. Our food had arrived, so maybe eight. Oh, wait. Alex got a phone call around that time. He took the call outside. While he was away from the table, I saw Rafe walk to the pub. You could check with Alex for the time of the call."

"Did you see Mr. Farraday leave?"

"No, but I suppose we might have missed him."

"And after dinner...?"

"We walked down to the river. That's where we were when we heard the sirens. We went back to Cottage Lane then."

Quimby must have been lightning fast at texting because he was tapping away with his thumbs, typing in what I'd told him. He finished and put his phone away. "Thank you, Ms. Sharp—"

Before he could wind up the conversation, I licked my lips and said, "Could you answer a question for me?"

"It depends on the question, I suppose."

"I have been helpful."

"Looking for a little *quid pro quo*, are you?" he said with a hint of a smile.

"Something like that. I did let you break into my cottage."

"All right, but no promises. I'll answer your question, if I can. I seem to remember you like to ask very pointed questions."

I shrugged. "I like to get things sorted out. Sometimes pointed questions are the only way to do it." I leaned forward. "It's about Rafe. The producer of the documentary has some...concerns... about him. Can you tell me if you think he's involved in the death of the woman?"

"As opposed to her turning up randomly in his cupboard?"

"Well, yes. I saw him this morning and asked him myself—a pointed question, if there ever was one. He said he didn't have anything to do with it, and I believed him."

"So you're taking a personal interest in my case, Ms. Sharp?"

I sighed. "The producer, Elise DuPont, assigned me the task of finding out if Rafe is guilty of...well, anything that would reflect badly on the production. The plan was to rely rather heavily on Rafe's interview as a hook for publicity, and she doesn't want to be burned."

"The notoriety of a possibly murdering scholar doesn't appeal to her?"

"No."

"Well, that's a first," Quimby said skeptically. "In my experience, television people jump at that sort of thing."

"Elise is not your normal television producer."

"Hmm. She asked you to question a possible murderer, and you trotted off and did it straight away?"

"No. She asked me to find out if he was involved. I saw him this morning while I was scouting a location and asked him. Now, I'm asking you."

Quimby ran his hand along the back of his neck. "He's involved. The victim was found in his burnt-out cottage, so yes, on that count. However, that's all I can say."

I sighed. "It was worth a shot."

"I can add that, in my professional experience, coincidences rarely happen."

"So you do think there is a link."

"No. I don't think anything. I'm gathering evidence, waiting to see what picture emerges." He removed a piece of paper from his pocket. "Do you recognize this woman?"

I took the sketch. "Yes. Yes, I do."

CHAPTER 8

QUIMBY HAD BEEN ON THE verge of standing, preparing to leave, but he went still. "Who is she?"

"Oh, I don't know who she is, but I saw her. Last night. She was walking along the path behind the cottage." I stared at the page a long moment then put it down on the kitchen table. It was like looking at someone's online avatar. It resembled the woman I'd seen in the lane, but in a cartoony way. "Her hair was not this dark, more blond," I added.

Quimby had his phone out again. "Tell me exactly what you saw."

"Not much. It was only a glance, but that's what she looked like. Alex and I stopped to watch the firefighters for a moment dealing with the fire in the trash bin then we walked on to the gate at the back of my garden. We stopped there and talked, deciding to meet in twenty minutes and go to the Chinese restaurant. He went on, and I opened the gate, but had trouble latching it closed. As I was struggling with it—it doesn't line up exactly—I looked up." I touched the corner of the paper. "She was walking along the path, and we made eye contact. It was a bit embarrassing, to tell you the truth, standing there, repeatedly closing the gate. I gave her a self-conscious smile. She returned it as she went by. I finally got the gate latched, and I went inside."

I felt a little sick, looking at the sketch. A few hours—no less than that—an hour and a half after I'd seen her, she was dead. And she'd died in such a horrible way. A chill crept over me, and I crossed my arms across my chest. "That poor woman."

"What was she wearing?"

I closed my eyes. "A pale green jacket—the waterproof kind. You know, athletic gear. Jeans and…" I trailed off and opened my eyes. "I don't remember her shoes or her shirt." My phone, which was on the table, rang. I didn't recognize the number and pushed the button to send the call to voicemail.

Quimby retrieved a plastic bag from another pocket. It contained a scrap of green material. "Similar to this?"

I took the bag and turned it over in my hands. "Yes, it was pastel, like this." Two edges of the fabric were stitched, but the third side was torn in a jagged pattern. The whole thing was only about an inch square. I handed the bag back to him. "Was she wearing this when you found her?"

"No. We weren't able to retrieve any of her clothing."

I closed my eyes again. Quimby kept talking. "This was caught under the threshold of the backdoor at Mr. Farraday's cottage." He pocketed the bag. "Keep that bit of information to yourself, please." His demeanor had changed. From the moment I said I'd seen the woman, he'd been completely serious. "Which direction was she walking?"

"She came from the village. When I left the gate, she was continuing along the path toward the cottages at the end of the lane and the woods."

"And Mr. Norcutt, was he still walking on the path as well?"

"Yes."

Quimby nodded and stood. "Do you know where Mr. Norcutt is now?"

I glanced at the time. "He's at Parkview Hall. They're shooting in the drawing room there today."

"All right. Thank you, Ms. Sharp. You've been very helpful. We've been working our way through the village, asking at the inn and at restaurants if anyone had seen her, but so far we hadn't turned up anything." He handed me a business card as he moved to the front door. "Give me a call, if you remember anything else about the woman. We'll need a formal statement from you later." He tapped the bolt as he opened the front door. "Keep these bolts locked when you're home," he said.

I returned to the kitchen table. The sketch sat on top of my Moleskine notebook. I grabbed it and hurried back to the front door, but Quimby was already gone. I picked up the business card and dialed his phone number. When he answered, I identified myself. "You left the sketch of the woman here."

"No worries. I also have it on my phone, but thanks for the call. Can you go to the church hall this afternoon and give your statement to Detective Sergeant Olney?"

"Yes, of course. I'll bring the sketch with me then."

"No need. We have plenty of them. You can bin it."

We ended our call, and I stared at the sketch, then folded it and put it inside the cover of my Moleskine. I couldn't throw the woman's picture away. It just didn't seem right.

I picked up my phone and called Alex. He didn't answer. I couldn't think of a quick way to summarize everything about my conversation with Quimby concerning the woman, so I only said, "DCI Quimby needs to talk with you. He's on his way to Parkview Hall now. Call me when you can."

I listened to the message from the call that had come in while Quimby was with me. It was Beatrice returning my call about a bookish location in the area. "Doug and Tara also own a nice little B & B, a renovated farmhouse with a charming study. They put large parties out there. You could check with them." She reeled off the number for the inn, which I jotted down in my notebook.

I hung up and dialed the number. Tara, Doug's wife, answered. I identified myself and told her we were looking for a possible location to shoot some interviews for the documentary. I described the look I would need and said Beatrice had mentioned a B & B they owned.

"Oh, yes, the West Farmhouse. It has a lovely little library. Quite nice. Shelves of antique books and an Adam fireplace. Doug is out there now, seeing to a repair in the kitchen. Would you like to see it now?"

"Yes, that would be wonderful."

She gave me directions, and I told her I'd go directly there. I hadn't sent off my scouting report yet, and I wanted it to have at least one other option besides Grove Cottage.

Fifteen minutes later, I turned the red MG onto a long drive and breathed a sigh of relief that the land surrounding the West Farmhouse was only gently rolling. No steep hills to navigate that would send the car seat flying back out of position.

The word farmhouse, to me, meant a frame house with a front porch set in a wide expanse of land. Farmhouses still existed in Southern California. I'd found several farmhouse-style locations for television shows and commercials once I got far enough out of Southern Cal's urban sprawl, and that was what I expected as I rolled to a stop in front of West Farmhouse, but it looked more like an upsized version of my cottage. Ivy covered the two-story stone building, and I could imagine a country squire living in it, and instead of working the land himself, he assigned that task to servants and tenant farmers.

I rolled to a stop beside a dirt-spotted station wagon. As I stepped out of the car, Doug came out the front door of the house, carrying a bucket and a trowel. "Tara called. You want to see the book room?"

"Yes, is this a good time?"

"Certainly. Come in." He put the bucket down on the step at the front door and waved me inside, wiping his hand on a white-spotted towel.

"We don't have any guests here today, so I was doing a spot of repair work. This way." He led me by a set of stairs finished in a dark wood with a matching bannister. I glimpsed a spacious kitchen with modern appliances and a long rectangular table under a wood-beamed ceiling before we reached a door. Doug stepped back so I could enter first.

"We converted the rest of the rooms to bedrooms, but kept this as a sitting room. Guests seem to like it."

"I can see why." The room was smaller and not nearly as extravagantly furnished as the study at Grove Cottage, but the room felt cozy. "What a wonderful place to curl up with a book," I said, pointing to the chairs on either side of the fireplace. White built-in bookshelves lined two walls, the fireplace with its delicate carvings and accents filled the third wall, and the last wall had large windows that overlooked the gently undulating green countryside. I already had my camera out. "Mind if I get a few photos?"

"Not at all. I'll be loading up the car."

I got to work, quickly getting the photos and notes I needed. I didn't want to keep Doug longer than was necessary. I put everything away and went to find Doug, thinking that if I was making the final decision, I'd pick the farmhouse room for the interview simply because I wouldn't have to work around Becca's finicky moods.

I found Doug in a small stone building around the side of the house filled with all sorts of maintenance equipment from mowers to paint brushes. "I'm done. Thank you so much. I'll let you know if the production is interested. Do you have any reservations coming up soon?"

"No, the family who booked it for this week cancelled. If I'd known a few days ago, you could have had a room."

"It would have been lovely, but a little far out of the village for me."

Doug stepped out of the building and secured a padlock on the door. "Still looking for locations?"

"Yes. We'd planned to use Lilac Cottage for an interview."

"I see. Sad business, that."

"Yes, it is."

"Do they know who she was?"

"No, not yet."

We walked around the side of the house to the cars. "Tara said the police came around with a sketch this morning, asking if the woman had stayed in the inn, but Tara didn't recognize her. Of course, Tara's been out of town lately. Her mum has been in hospital."

"I'm sorry to hear that."

"She's fine now." He pulled out a set of keys. "Well, I best lock up and get down to the church hall. They want me to look at the sketch as well."

"Oh, I can save you a trip." I took the sketch out of my notebook and handed it to him. "Quimby came by my cottage today and left that."

Doug unfolded the paper and gave it a cursory look, then his gaze sharpened. He patted his pocket and removed a pair of glasses. "Well, I'll be."

"Do you recognize her?"

"Yes. She stayed here." He pointed his thumb over his shoulder at the farmhouse. "Came with a big group for the bike ride last weekend." He ran his hand down over his mouth as he shook his head. "Awful to think she's dead now."

"I know. I feel the same way. I saw her, too."

"But you weren't here last weekend."

"No, it was yesterday, walking down the lane behind the cottages."

91

"Hmm. I wonder why she came back? And where did she stay this time?"

"Well, the police will be able to track her down now. You'll have her details."

Doug was still working his hand up and down along the side of his mouth. "I don't think so. One person from the group reserved the whole farmhouse, and it wasn't her. A biking club, coming in for the race. I'll only have the one person's information."

"Still, that's a start," I said. "I'm sure the police can check with that person and track her down.

"Yes. Well, I better get on." He held out the sketch, but I waved him off.

"No, you keep it. You can give it to the police. Thank you for letting me photograph the room. I'll let you know if they're interested."

Doug climbed the steps to lock up the farmhouse, and I drove away, his words echoing in my head. Why had the woman returned to Nether Woodsmoor so soon after her visit last weekend? The bike race that Doug mentioned must have been the one Alex had told me about. If she came to the village for that, why return so quickly? More bike riding? To meet someone? Had she forgotten something?

My phone buzzed with a text. I stopped at the end of the farmhouse's lane to read it. It was from Elise's assistant, Mary. *Do you have the scouting report for new interview locations?*

Yes. I'll send it to you within the hour, I texted back and headed back to the cottage. Time to put thoughts of the unknown woman out of my mind and focus on my job.

I finished the report and sent it off with five minutes to spare. I leaned back in the kitchen chair and stretched my arms over my head, debating if I should go to Parkview Hall. I checked my phone. No response from Alex, which seemed odd. Well, I wasn't his keeper. He didn't have to check in with me, I reasoned, but I couldn't help but feel a tiny bit miffed. He had been flirting with me. I knew it. And I was flirting back. I blew out a sigh. I wasn't great at this relationship stuff. I always got tripped up along the way.

Lori, the starry-eyed intern at my old job, used to tell me I was too picky and that I couldn't shove love into a spreadsheet. But Lori fell in and out of love on a near hourly basis, so I wasn't sure she was the best person to take advice from. Besides, there was nothing wrong with having a plan and some standards. I hadn't had time to date much during the last few years, but when I had, this was usually about the point that things sputtered and died. Meet guy. Find out more about him. Go on a few dates. And then I'd begin second-guessing and analyzing everything he said and did along with everything *I* said and did, which made me more self-conscious and nervous, which the guys seemed to pick up on. It was a vicious circle. *Enough. I was doing it again. Thinking too much.*

I flipped my Moleskine notebook closed and returned the memory card to my camera then packed everything away in my tote bag. I would head over to Parkview Hall, but first I needed food. I'd only had a cup of coffee this morning at the inn. I'd worked straight through lunch while finishing up the scouting report, and now I was starving.

I didn't even bother opening the old-fashioned refrigerator. I knew there literally wasn't a thing to eat because I still hadn't gone shopping. Time to fix that. If I was going to settle in here in Nether Woodsmoor, I couldn't continue to eat out every meal. At least not if I wanted to continue to fit into the small number of clothes I'd brought with me. I slipped my phone and some cash into my jeans pocket then left through the back garden.

I'd had enough of driving on the wrong side of the road for

one day. I needed to walk, get out in the fresh air. I could have walked along Cottage Lane to get to the small grocery store a few blocks away, but the more rural-feeling path that ran along the back of the cottages tempted me.

I hesitated for a second at the back gate, thinking of the woman found in Rafe's cottage. She'd walked along this path shortly before she died. A few bikers whizzed by me, and I saw one other walker in the distance, a serious one. She had walking poles and was huffing along at a quick pace as she came toward me from the village. In the other direction, just past Alex's cottage, five or six people were repairing a section of the dry stone wall. A pile of the flat stones that had been in the wall had fallen onto the path. I could hear the faint clinks and thuds of the stones knocking against each other as the group fitted them back into the wall.

I saw the man that Alex had introduced to me at the pub hefting one of the flat stones. I couldn't remember his name. Henry? Harry? No, neither of those. He saw me and gave me a nod of acknowledgement. I raised a hand then stepped through the gate and worked to latch it back into place. The path wasn't deserted. There was no need to be worried.

I breathed in deeply as I walked toward Nether Woodsmoor. The sun filtered through the tree branches that were mostly still bare. The bits of sky I could see through the oak branches were vibrantly blue and the day was warm, but not too hot. Ivy climbed up the dry stone walls that edged both sides of the path, and here and there a spray of honeysuckle tumbled over the wall from the cottages' back gardens. It was a picture perfect day on the outskirts of an English village. The beauty of nature soothed me. It always did. This landscape was so different from the rugged hills around Southern California or the waves of the Pacific, but being outdoors worked its magic on me. The transition to a new place and a new job, Elise's hostility, the fire, the poor woman who had died—all those things were still there in the background, but the knot of stress inside me seemed to loosen a bit as I strode along.

I came to the parking area for the bike path and cut through it into Nether Woodsmoor. The parking area was empty except for a few cars, which I supposed wasn't that unusual since it was the middle of the work week. I edged between a gray Volvo with a bike rack and a silver hatchback then stopped to consult the map posted on the sign at the trail head, which besides having the trail map on it, also had a few of Nether Woodsmoor's streets.

I got my bearings and continued down the narrow sloping street that ran from the parking area into Nether Woodsmoor. After two more blocks, I reached the grocery store. It was like the library, a stone building on the outside, but totally refurbished and modern on the inside. Not a wooden beam in sight. I picked up a hand basket and collected the basics: coffee, cereal, milk, bread, ham and roast beef for sandwiches, and some fruit. I grabbed a package of spaghetti and red sauce, figuring that would be enough of a load to get back to the cottage. I went to the checkout, thinking that perhaps I should have driven Alex's car after all. I sat my basket down on the conveyer belt and began to unload it, half-listening to the cashier and the customer in front of me as they chatted.

"Having a nice dinner, are we?" the cashier said in a flirty voice.

"Oh no, nothing special," the customer replied, and I looked up. It was Rafe, swiping his credit card through the payment slot.

The cashier, a pretty middle-aged woman, scanned a bottle of wine and set it down beside a package of steaks, a bundle of asparagus, and a long loaf of bread. She made a tsking sound. "Go on with you. Steak and wine." She put the items in a reusable carrier bag. "I'd like to have a *nothing special* dinner like that."

"Perhaps we should dine together," Rafe said, a teasing grin on his face.

The cashier tilted her head. "My husband would have something to say about that, I'm sure."

Rafe winked. "That's a shame."

The cashier gave him one last smile and turned to me. Rafe glanced my way, then did a double-take. "Well, hello. I didn't see you there. Stocking up?"

The cashier passed my cereal and milk over the scanner. "Yes. My cupboard was literally bare. How's the…um…writing going?"

"Excellent." He stuffed the receipt in his pocket and picked up the bag. "Just taking a break. I've got to get right back at it."

I nodded. Rafe said good-bye and turned to leave, but the cashier called out. "Oh, that timer you wanted. We got some in this morning."

"Timer?"

"Yes, for the lights."

"Oh, right. Thanks. I'll get one next time." Rafe raised his hand with the bag, a good-bye gesture, and paced away quickly.

I added two reusable shopping bags to my pile of items so I could carry everything back to the cottage and noticed the cashier wasn't nearly as friendly to me as she'd been to Rafe. I retraced my route back to the cottage, again going through the parking area at the bike path, nodding a greeting to the riders who were stowing their bikes on the rack of their Volvo. To give them plenty of space, I walked around the other car and continued up to the walking path, enjoying the birds flitting through the lattice of tree branches overhead and then swooping down into the bushes and hedgerows, which were covered in tiny buds. But at the back of my mind was the image of Rafe chatting so casually with the cashier. He didn't appear to have a care in the world.

By the time I got to my cottage, the straps of the carrier bags were cutting into my fingers, but I was glad I'd walked. The scenery was worth it, and it felt good to get a little exercise. The group working on the stone wall was gone, and the repair was complete. The wall was straight and true, the flat rocks positioned in an interlocking pattern and held in place by larger, rounder stones placed atop the flat ones. A small sign perched over the wall where they'd been working. I walked over and read it. "Repaired by the Nether Woodsmoor Historical Society."

I turned away and entered the back garden. Elise would probably not approve of me running to the store during the day, but I hadn't taken a lunch break. I slapped together a sandwich and ate it while tapping out emails to my mother and several friends in California. I kept my messages breezy and general, avoiding any mention of the murder next door. Thankfully, my mother only remembered what she wanted to remember. She was upset with me for moving (even temporarily) out of her potential matchmaking zone, and had waved me off or had changed the subject anytime I tried to talk to her about the job in England, firmly believing that if she didn't acknowledge the subject, it wouldn't happen. She had probably also blocked out the name of the village where I was working, so I wasn't worried that she'd hear about the murder, not that a death in a small English village would make the news in Southern California anyway.

I cleared up my dishes, sent a text to Mary and copied Elise on it, informing them that I had to stop by the church hall and sign a statement for the police, then I'd be on my way to Parkview Hall. I sent another text to Alex, telling him I would have his MG back at Parkview Hall soon. I double-checked my messages, but there was nothing from him. I put my phone away with a frown and steeled myself to concentrate on driving.

I zipped through Nether Woodsmoor and actually took the correct exit at the roundabout, which dropped me off at the church. I found a parking area in the back and wedged the MG into a slot among rows of dark sedans. The red sports car stood out like a pimple.

The church hall, which was in a separate building from the church with its towering spire, reminded me of a location shoot.

Extension cords and phone wires snaked across the hardwood floor between several almost bare tables, each with only a computer and phone. No photos or posters, or personal mementos. A general air of bustle and movement filled the place, echoing up to the high ceiling as chairs squeaked, voices murmured on the phone, and footsteps tapped quickly across the floor. It had the atmosphere of temporary activity that permeated film sets. A few days and the whole thing could be dismantled and gone.

I gave my name to the man seated at a table positioned directly in front of the door and said, "I need to sign my statement about the woman I saw in the lane behind my cottage, the woman who died." He directed me to a row of chairs lining the wall and said someone would be with me in a moment. The man who'd been working on the stone wall was seated in a chair pulled up to a table near me. On the other side of the table from him, a woman in uniform asked him, "What time did you arrive at the pub?"

I was surprised that the police were interviewing people in the main room, but Nether Woodsmoor was a small village. The church hall was probably the biggest building in town. I guessed they were making do with what they had. I supposed I'd be next up to fill the chair after the man left. I cast about trying to remember the guy's name. Harold? Howard, maybe? I couldn't call him the Stone Wall Guy.

I wasn't used to remembering my neighbor's names. In California, I barely knew my neighbor's faces. The rotation in and out of the apartment community was as constant as a revolving door, and a general wave or half-smile of greeting at the communal mailbox sufficed, but Nether Woodsmoor was a smaller, more settled community. I needed to work on putting names to faces. I leaned forward as subtly as possible so I could listen in better. Perhaps the woman would mention the man's name.

"I'm not sure. Probably between seven-thirty and seven-forty-five."

"And was Mr. Farraday at the pub when you arrived?"

"No, I saw him come in later."

"How much later?"

"Honestly, I have no idea. I didn't look at my watch. I would guess it was probably around eight."

"Thank you, Mr. Lyons. I'll print this up and have you sign it. If you'll give me a moment."

I leaned back in my chair. Hector Lyons, that was it. Such a dramatic, heroic name. It seemed a bit of a mismatch for the slender, washed out man with his hair and beard fading from blond to gray.

An exterior door at the side of the room opened. Quimby strode in and the atmosphere changed slightly. It was as if everyone sat up a little straighter and focused more ardently on their tasks. Quimby quickly consulted with a few people around the room, spotted me, and headed across the floor in my direction. "Ms. Sharp, is Mr. Norcutt here?"

"No."

"But that is his MG in the car park?"

"Yes. I drove it here. He let me borrow it today." I stood up. "He wasn't at Parkview Hall?"

"No, I haven't been able to reach him. I went out there and was told he'd gone to Upper Benning to fetch another generator. How did he get to Upper Benning?"

"The production has several rental cars. He probably used one of those," I explained.

"Have you been in contact with him today?"

"No, I left him a message, but haven't heard back."

Quimby's eyebrows squished down into a frown. "Please let me know if you hear from him."

A man broke into our conversation. "Excuse me, sir." Eagerness pulsed through his words. "I think I've found her."

CHAPTER 9

QUIMBY AND THE OTHER MAN moved a few steps away as another voice drew my attention. "Ms. Sharp? This way please. We can take care of your statement now."

I looked over and found Olney waiting for me. He'd worked with Quimby on the previous case I'd been involved in, and I'd talked to him a few times.

He could easily have slipped onto the film set. He would have fit in, appearance-wise, among the talent. He was one of the Beautiful People and looked like leading man material straight from central casting—tall, broad-shouldered, square jaw, brilliant blue eyes under a swath of black hair, and a killer smile. He was so good-looking that you had to stare at him a moment or two, while you wondered what he was doing walking around with all of us normal, average-looking people.

I blinked and pulled myself together. "Oh, right." I looked around as I followed Olney to a nearby table. The female investigator I'd assumed would talk to me still huddled with Hector Lyons.

Olney gestured me to a seat on the far side of a table. "DCI

Quimby sent me the details of your statement earlier. I've got it typed up. Let me print it then you can go over it."

As I sat down to wait, Quimby and the other man strode over to a table beside me.

"What have you got?" Quimby asked him.

The man tapped the computer screen. "Amy Brown," he said, his voice carrying in his excitement. "Resident of Manchester. Came down with her local cycling group and stayed in the West Farmhouse B & B. Works at a software development company. She took off work early yesterday and hadn't been in today. No holiday scheduled and hasn't called in."

"Good work," Quimby said.

"It was just a matter of checking each one of the names on the cycling group's registration. She's the only one who hasn't turned up at work today."

"Get the details over to the medical examiner's office. Morriston will want to get on those dental records straight away. Next of kin?"

"None listed that I can find. Possibly an orphan?"

"Hmm. Keep checking. What about transportation? How did she get here? She had a driving license." He pointed at the screen. "Any record of a vehicle registration?"

"Yes. A gray Citroen DS3."

"All right. Let's sweep the parking areas again. There's no train service here, so she either drove in or took the bus. If we don't find anything, we'll move the search outward from here. You coordinate that. Pull Hicks and Dooly in to help you."

I heard a familiar voice and looked over my shoulder. Alex stood at the table near the door. I raised my hand and caught his eye. The officer waved him to the chairs and went back to his paperwork. Alex came through the desks toward me.

"I was getting worried about you," I said. "I called you and sent a text."

"I can't find my phone. I think it might be in the car."

I pulled the keys out of my pocket. "Here. I've had my fill of driving today. I guess you've heard the police want to talk to you?"

"Yes, I got the message as soon as I got back to Parkview Hall. Let me get my phone. I'll be right back," Alex said, turning away.

"Mr. Norcutt," a voice said sharply and heads across the room looked toward Quimby, who closed the short distance between himself and Alex, his long strides quick and purposeful. "We've been trying to reach you."

"Yes. Sorry about that. I lost my phone. It may be in my car, which I lent to Kate today. I was on my way to check." He held up the keys.

"A few questions for you first."

"It won't take a moment," Alex said easily.

"It will have to wait." Quimby's expression was serious and his manner reserved and formal.

Alex pocketed the keys and matched Quimby's frosty tone. "All right. How can I help you?"

"First, what were you discussing with Ms. Sharp?" Quimby asked.

"My phone and the fact that you wanted to see me."

"What else?" Quimby asked.

"Nothing."

Quimby looked at me, eyebrows raised.

"Yes, that's all. I said I'd tried to call him, and he said he thought his phone might be in the car so I gave him the keys."

Quimby's gaze bobbed back and forth from Alex's face to mine. "Mr. Norcutt, if you'll come with me." He turned. Alex sent me a puzzled look before following him. Olney was coming back through the tables toward me, holding several sheets of A4 paper. Quimby had a word with him then directed Alex to an interior door at the back of the room.

Olney gave me the statement to read then went directly to the man positioned at the front door and talked to him quietly. Both of their glances strayed to me once, and I quickly focused on my statement with the feeling that the guy up front was in trouble for letting Alex talk to me instead of keeping us separate, which sent a little spark of worry through me. Why would they care if Alex and I talked about his phone?

I shook my head and focused on reading through my statement. I finished, signed it, and handed it over to Olney. He asked about what Alex and I had talked about as well. "His lost phone."

Olney nodded, made a note in a small notebook, and then told me I could leave.

"I'll wait for Alex."

"That's fine. You can have a seat along the wall."

It was a long wait. The noise level in the room dropped. Several officers had left—probably out searching Nether Woodsmoor for Amy Brown's car—and Hector had left. It felt like it was near closing time at an office, but I wondered if they actually closed down. Maybe they ran twenty-four/seven with a smaller number of officers during the night hours.

At the thirty-minute mark, the door opened and Alex emerged, a shell-shocked look on his face. He came toward me slowly, walking as if he had been given horrible news. Quimby was a few steps behind him, but caught up and passed him, coming straight to me.

"One more question, Ms. Sharp."

"Okay," I said cautiously.

"This way." He motioned me toward the door where he'd taken Alex.

I hesitated then moved toward it. When my path crossed Alex's, I paused. Quimby made as if to intervene, but I said quickly to Alex, "You'll wait for me here?"

"What?" He blinked and focused on me.

"Quimby has another question for me. Will you wait for me here?"

"Yes. Yes, of course," Alex said.

The door led to a short hallway with two offices. Quimby took me to the first one on the right, indicated a visitor's chair then moved behind the desk, which was covered with files, papers, and a map. He scooted his chair close to the desk, linked his fingers together, and rested them on the pile of paper. "Why didn't you tell us about the length of Mr. Norcutt's phone call?"

My mind was full of lost cell phones. "What call? He'd lost his phone."

"Not today. Last evening during your dinner."

"Oh. But I did tell you about it. He got a call and stepped outside."

"And was gone for around ten minutes, he estimates. Would you agree on the time frame?"

"Yes," I said reluctantly. I had a bad feeling about this.

"That is a long time for a dinner partner to be gone. Why didn't you mention it?" He tapped the paper with my signature.

"Honestly? You didn't ask me how long he was gone," I said carefully, thinking back to when Quimby had been in my cottage earlier today. "You wanted to know about Rafe. I was more focused on trying to remember things related to him. I thought you were interested in his movements."

"Yes, we were at that time." His slight emphasis on the word *were* had me frowning.

"You were interested, but you're not now—" I broke off as the penny dropped. They'd eliminated Rafe. "You mean Rafe isn't a suspect?"

Quimby's face shuttered, and I fell back against the chair. "His alibi checked out? He was at the library all afternoon?"

"I'm afraid I can't share that type of information with you, Ms. Sharp." He went into some spiel about thanking me for coming in, but I wasn't listening.

"The library and the pub. Of course you'd verify it," I murmured to myself. "And I was the one who saw him walk directly from the library to the pub." Had my words somehow shifted the investigation from Rafe to Alex?

I leaned forward on the seat, interrupting Quimby's rote speech. "You can't seriously think that *Alex* had something to do with that woman's death."

Quimby gazed back at me, his face noncommittal. "Be careful, Ms. Sharp."

"But Alex? He's kind and helpful and considerate. He would never—"

Quimby stood and buttoned his suit coat. "Appearances can be deceiving, Ms. Sharp. I've met some very charming murderers."

WHEN I EMERGED from the doorway back into the central part of the church hall, I probably looked as stunned as Alex had. He was sitting on one of the chairs by the wall, bent over with his elbows on his knees and his hands on either side of his forehead.

I touched his shoulder. "Alex."

He jerked upright, then sighed. "Oh, it's you. I was afraid they might keep you back there a long time."

I swallowed. "No, I told Quimby everything I could think of earlier today."

He stood up. "I'm a suspect." I could tell the shock of it had worn off a bit, but he still looked shaken.

"I know." I sighed. "And I think it might be my fault."

"What?"

I closed my eyes, trying to think where to start. When I opened them, I noticed the female investigator who had been talking to Hector suddenly became very busy with some papers on her table. "Not here."

"Yeah, let's get out of here while they'll still let me leave," Alex said with a wan smile.

He pushed the heavy door open, and I breathed in the scent of freshly cut grass. As the door thudded closed behind us, I asked, "Do we need to go back to Parkview Hall?"

"No, they'll have wrapped for today."

"Then let's get some food. The White Duck?"

Alex nodded, and we didn't speak again until we were ensconced at a table in the rear of the pub, our chairs pulled around next to each other so we could both have our backs to the wall, like two cornered animals setting up to defend themselves from attackers.

We'd placed our order at the bar on our way to the table, and now I took a sip of my water. I certainly didn't need any caffeine to stay awake now. I was shocked into total alertness.

Alex had a pint in front of him, but he wasn't drinking it, only staring into it. "I don't understand what's happened. All Quimby's questions revolved around what I did last night. He obviously thinks I'm involved some way in that woman's death, but I don't see—I just don't get it."

I blew out a breath. "It's because of what I saw and the timing. Did Quimby show you the sketch of the woman who died?"

"No, not a sketch. A photograph." Alex ran his finger around the base of his mug. I could tell he was not paying that much attention to what I was saying, which was not like him at all. He was usually so attentive and observant.

"Oh, right," I said. "Probably her driver's license photo. I overheard one of the men talking to Quimby. Sounds like they're pretty sure it was a woman named Amy Brown."

"Yes, that was the name he asked me about, but I don't know any Amy Brown."

"Well, I didn't know her, but I saw her." He stopped staring at his mug and gave me his full attention. The force of his gaze, the intensity of his attention, was like having a spotlight turned on me.

"What? How could you?" Alex asked. "Quimby said she was from Manchester. You know people in Manchester?"

"No, but I saw her. She was on the path behind the cottages last night. I saw her after we'd seen the fire in the trash bin. As I was closing the gate—trying to close the gate, the latch wouldn't work—I saw her walking from the village toward your cottage. We exchanged a glance, then I went inside."

"And she was found dead in Rafe's cottage...what? A little over an hour later?"

"Yes." I took a sip of my water and went on, "I think you must have been one of the last people to see her alive."

"But I *didn't* see her."

"Well, to be seen with her, then," I amended miserably. "Alex, I'm sorry about this. If I hadn't said something to Quimby today..."

Alex put a hand on my arm. "No. Don't do that to yourself. You had to tell him what you saw. If she was on that path at the same time I was, of course they're going to ask me about it, but what I don't understand is why the intense questioning?" He shrugged and leaned back in the chair. "I don't know—maybe I'm being paranoid. Maybe Quimby questions everyone like that. But I got the distinct feeling that I was at the top of his list of possible suspects." He ran his hands through his hair. "And all because I ran back to the cottage during dinner."

"You went back to the cottage?" I asked.

"I couldn't remember if I'd closed Slink's pet door. She's learned she can jump the back wall, so I've been keeping it closed when I'm not home. I came home twice last week and found her sniffing around the back lane. And then with all the weird stuff going on in the neighborhood, I figured safe was better than sorry." He shook his head. "But that puts me right there during the time she died. It must. If you saw her on the path around seven, she had to have died between seven and whatever time the fire started. I didn't look at my watch after dinner, but it couldn't have been later than eight or eight-fifteen when we heard the sirens."

"Yes, I'm pretty sure that's what the police think. Quimby was very interested in how long you were gone from the restaurant. Did you see anyone else?"

Alex pushed his untouched drink away. "That was Quimby's next question, too. No, unfortunately, I didn't see anyone else." He shifted in his chair. "This may sound callous, but what I don't understand is, why aren't they interested in Rafe? She was found in his cottage—not mine. Did he know her? Who knows, maybe they've asked him the same things, too."

"They have. Quimby was at Becca's house this morning when I went to talk to Rafe about scouting locations for the interview. Becca didn't want to talk to me right away, so she left me in the morning room, which was located not too far from where Quimby was asking Rafe questions."

"You eavesdropped."

"The windows were open," I said defensively.

"I wasn't criticizing. What did you hear?"

"Rafe says he didn't know her and that he was in the Nether Woodsmoor library all afternoon then went directly to the pub. I actually saw him walk from the library to the pub while you were gone. I'm sorry. I really wish I hadn't been so helpful, but I felt so bad for that poor woman. I had no idea that it would all circle back to you like this."

"You couldn't have known. And you did the right thing, telling them everything you knew."

Louise moved through the tables and dropped off our food. I mostly pushed the lettuce in my salad around. I didn't have much of an appetite, and I noticed that Alex only ate about half of his sandwich before he pushed his plate away.

Louise boxed up my unfinished salad for what she called "take away," but Alex shook his head when she offered to do the same for him. We left the pub and headed back to the church where the

MG was parked. The lights were still on in the church hall, but there were only a few cars left in the lot.

We climbed in the car, and Alex shifted the driver's seat all the way to the back setting.

"Oh, did you know that seat is broken? It doesn't completely lock out if you move it closer to the steering wheel."

"No, I had no idea."

"Yeah, I figured you always drove with it pushed all the way back." I related how I'd discovered the issue in as light a way as I could since Alex was already stressed out. "Elise may be right. Driving may not be the best thing for me, just yet."

"I'm sure if you can find a car with a seat that doesn't fly backward unexpectedly you'll do great. Sounds like you did fine even with the flying seat. Sorry about that. I had no idea. Another thing to add to the repair list. I think the MG keeps the garage in Nether Woodsmoor afloat."

Alex turned the car at Cottage Lane. "You can just drop me here," I said as he rolled to a stop in front of my cottage.

"Do you want me to check in with you in the morning—" he broke off and began looking around the console. "My phone. I didn't even think about it again after that session with Quimby." He reached down to pat around under the seat. "Ah." He straightened, the phone in his hand. "It must have slipped down there this morning." He checked the display and let out a low whistle. "I had no idea I was so popular."

"What time do we start tomorrow?"

"Six. Want to ride with me?"

"Yes, please."

"Okay. So I'll see you at five-thirty."

I opened the door, then paused before I got out. "I'm sure everything with the investigation will work out. These things linking you to Amy Brown, they're all circumstantial. You were on the same path shortly before she died, and you went back to the cottage during that time. In the big scope of things, that's nothing. I'm sure the police will turn up other connections. She's got to have some reason for being in Nether Woodsmoor on a Tuesday afternoon, if she lived and worked in Manchester. I'm sure the police will find some other link and move on from you."

"I hope you're right."

CHAPTER 10

*R*AIN WAS FORECAST FOR THURSDAY, and despite the sky over Nether Woodsmoor being clear in the early morning, a layer of gray clouds hovered on the western horizon. Elise had juggled the schedule and moved the day's activities indoors to Coventry House.

I loved Coventry House. A three-storied, gabled home with ivy and mullioned windows, it was surrounded by a pleasant garden with graveled paths, evergreen shrubs, and low boxwoods. Inside, it had classic lines with wainscoting and symmetrical design in both the layout as well as in the placement of windows and other decorative elements such as bookcases and fireplaces. With the eclectic mix of classical furnishing tossed together with more modern pieces it really had felt like a family home—exactly what we'd wanted for Longbourn when we scouted for the feature film. But now that the film was off the table, the owner was still delighted with the idea of his home being used as a film location and was on-board for the documentary. Alex had told me during our ride to work this morning that the owner was away on a trip with his daughter to the south of

France, and while I missed him, I hoped that he was enjoying his vacation.

Instead of playing the role of Longbourn, as Alex and I had originally envisioned, Coventry House was now slated to stand-in for Jane Austen's home. The documentary was recreating scenes from Austen's novels as well as scenes depicting her life. The interior of Coventry House was to play the part of Jane Austen's childhood home, the Steventon rectory, which was torn down after Austen's father retired and the family moved to Bath.

I hovered in the hallway outside the drawing room where the actress portraying our young Jane Austen was seated at a delicate desk near a window, scribbling in a notebook, pausing to look out the window occasionally. I hadn't seen the room since the original scouting trip a month earlier. It now looked completely different. Every modern piece of furniture or decoration was gone, and the room had been transformed into a Regency-appropriate space with furniture with classical lines. This morning, the actors portraying Jane's sister Cassandra as well as her brothers, had replicated scenes of the Austen family's evenings. Austen often read her stories aloud to her family or participated in plays the whole family acted out.

During a break in filming, Melissa came over to me, carrying two cups. Today she had on a pair of worn jeans and an over-sized sweatshirt with the words *Calm Down* printed in a huge font. She held out one cup. "I figured you'd rather have coffee than tea. Was I right?"

"Oh, yes. Thanks."

"It's black."

"Perfect."

"Don't thank me yet. I do have an ulterior motive. What's this I hear about Alex being questioned by the police?"

Alex was at Parkview Hall this morning, supervising the transformation of the drawing room back to its normal state.

He'd dropped me at Coventry House this morning and driven on to Parkview Hall.

"How do you know about that?" I sipped the coffee, which wasn't gourmet by a long shot, but it was caffeine.

"Are you kidding? Film set. Incestuous, insular community. Everyone knows about it."

"Of course. Yes, they did talk to Alex, but they talked to me too. Routine stuff," I said in an effort to downplay any rumors that were circulating.

"Oh good. Felix is running around telling everyone that Alex is a prime suspect—says that he heard someone say that they saw Alex talking to this mysterious woman—or some such rubbish and that you saw the woman before she died."

"Oh—I, ah—"

Melissa had been about to take a drink from her cup, but her hand stilled. "You're not serious," she said, correctly reading my fumbling reaction. "You saw her?"

I sighed. It didn't seem like it would do any good to deny it now. "Yes, but only a glimpse of her on the path behind my cottage. That's it."

"Wow—a rumor that was actually true. Well, at least that means that the part about Alex has to be way off base," she said, watching me closely.

I sighed and shook my head, deciding I couldn't fool Melissa.

"No," she said, amazement filling her voice. "They can't think that Alex had anything to do with it? Alex? That's crazy. He's one of the nicest, sweetest guys around. There's no way…"

"I agree," I said, glad to know that someone else shared an opinion the opposite of Quimby's.

"But why? Why would they think that about Alex?"

"He had the bad luck to go to his cottage during the critical time. Alone."

"Oh, well, that's nothing. They don't have anyone else to hassle now, do they?" She patted my arm. "Don't look so worried.

He'll be fine. The police will turn up some new leads, and they'll forget all about him." She turned and leaned a shoulder against the wall. "Did you see that hunky sergeant? I wouldn't mind if he interviewed me," she said with a waggle of her eyebrows.

My phone buzzed, and Melissa gave me a wave as I moved outside to take the call. I recognized Jeff's number. He was working security. I'd met him Tuesday when he called me to help deal with a disgruntled neighbor during the Parkview Hall day of filming. "Yeah, Jeff. What's up?"

"Got an issue at the back of the garden, a group of ramblers. They want to cut through the woods to Parkview Hall."

"No, they can't do that. Those woods are in view from the drawing room where we're filming today. I'll be right there." I shrugged into my yellow raincoat, glad I'd made room for it in my suitcase, and pulled a local map from my tote bag. I'd picked up several maps from a display in the pub.

I went out the front door and around to the side of the house opposite from where they were filming then cut through the garden. I moved across the wide lawn that stretched to a gate with an arch of shrubbery over it. While I'd been inside during the morning, the clouds had slid in overhead and now the day was overcast, and a fine mist of drizzle filled the air. I slipped outside the gate and found Jeff blocking a group of about five hikers, who were bundled in waterproof jackets and sturdy shoes.

I approached the group. "I understand you want to get to Parkview Hall?"

A woman stepped forward, blinking as the drizzle hit her eyes. "Ah, American. That explains it. You obviously don't understand. You can't stop us from walking that way, no matter what this burly chap here says. You can't block these footpaths. They are rights-of-way, going back hundreds of years—"

"Yes, I understand that," I interrupted her as she took a deep breath, preparing to launch into a lecture. "I love the footpaths, too. One of my favorite things about the countryside, but I'm afraid that today you can't go down this one." Dealing with people wasn't exactly my strongest suit, but I'd learned long ago that jumping in and agreeing with someone usually put the brakes on their anger, at least temporarily.

I explained about the filming and the permits and the temporary nature of the closure, then I whipped out the map and said, "Let's see if there's another way to get to Parkview Hall that avoids this stretch of wood. You're probably more familiar with reading these maps than I am..." I trailed off, and after a short internal struggle, she gave in to her desire to demonstrate her superior map-reading skills and bent over the paper with me. Within a few minutes, she'd found an alternate route, and they departed. They weren't exactly happy with the situation, but I'd managed to smooth things over enough that they had moved on.

I made my way back across the wide lawn, circling around a huge oak tree with a rope swing. I was still twenty or thirty feet from the house when the drizzle increased to a light rain and began to patter and plop in big splotches onto my shoulders. I would be soaked before I reached the house. I cut sideways, closer to the towering tree to give me a little more cover. At the same moment I dodged under a low-hanging branch, a bee zipped by. *That was weird.* I didn't know bees flew when it rained. I paused, my hand against the rough bark of the tree trunk as I pulled up the hood of my raincoat.

Another bee zipped through the air near my ear, then a bit of bark near my cheek exploded. Instinctively, I ducked, knowing that those weren't bees. *Bullets? No, it couldn't be—*

Another projectile whizzed through the air and more bark went flying. Yes, bullets, apparently.

I scrambled around to the other side of the tree. I peeked around the tree trunk toward the thick hedges that enclosed the lawn in the direction the shots had come from.

I didn't see anyone. The hedges weren't fully in leaf, but the branches were dense and I couldn't tell in my quick glance if someone was on the other side of the hedges. Beyond the hedges, a belt of woodland stretched darkly up a gradual rise of land.

I turned back toward Coventry House and scanned the wide expanse of green lawn. Moving in any direction would expose me to full view of the hedge and the wood. I tensed, expecting to hear the high-pitched whine of another bullet, but it was quiet except for the patter of rain splashing into the growing puddles on the lawn and pattering onto the tree branches.

"Kate!"

I jumped and looked toward the front of the house, where Paul, the A.D., was trotting my way with an open umbrella hefted overhead.

"No, don't come closer. Someone is shooting."

"What?" Paul removed the pencil from behind his ear and shook his head as he closed the distance. "I thought you said something about someone *shooting* at you." His tone said he thought it was a great joke, but as he came to a stop beside me and took in my expression, he said, "You're serious?"

"Yes, unless those were kamikaze bees embedding themselves on the other side of the tree."

"Kate, I think you're—" He held the umbrella over me as he took a step away to look at the bark on the other side of the tree.

I gripped his arm and pulled him back. "Don't do that."

He came back to stand beside me, his face white. "There's a bullet embedded in the bark."

"Yes, I know." I had my phone out. "I'm calling Jeff."

He nodded. "Brilliant idea."

CHAPTER 11

"*W*E RECOVERED TWO BULLETS FROM the tree." Quimby said half an hour later as he sat down across the table from me in the modern and completely updated kitchen of Coventry House—we wouldn't be filming in there—or anywhere else for that matter today. Jeff and the other security guys had swept the area around Coventry House all the way up into the woods and hadn't found anyone, but the production had to shut down while the police investigated.

I wrapped my hands around a mug of tea. Someone had brought it to me. I didn't remember who. It was still pouring, the rain hammering down on the room and sluicing through the gutters.

Elise had been livid, so angry that she couldn't get any words out. I only had a fleeting glimpse of her as Jeff escorted me and Paul into the kitchen on Quimby's orders, but that one glance had been enough. Quimby had already been in and talked to Paul and me once. We'd given him the highlights of what had happened. Olney had appeared in the doorway, asking for Paul to go with him, and I'd wondered momentarily if Melissa had been able to snag Olney's attention.

"So let's go through this again," Quimby said, bringing my attention back to him. "You took the call from Jeff Hayes," he paused to consult his notes. "At two-twelve."

"Yes, if that's what my phone log shows, then that's right. I didn't notice the time."

"So you spoke to the walkers and then you left the garden gate?" I nodded, and he said, "Tell me what happened."

I sighed. "I've told you already. It started raining, coming down really hard, and I headed for the tree to get some shelter. "I heard what I thought was a bee buzz by me, which I thought was strange—that bees would be flying around in heavy rain, I mean —but what do I know about bees?" The corners of Quimby's mouth turned up a fraction. I went on, "I stopped moving for a second to put up the hood of my raincoat."

"That coat there?" Quimby asked, pointing to the yellow rain-coat, which was draped over another chair.

"Yes. That's mine."

Quimby shook his head. "That color makes a heck of a target. Go on."

I tried not to think about someone looking through a viewfinder at my yellow raincoat. "That's when I heard the noise again. A bit of bark sort of exploded and that's when I knew it wasn't a bee. I think I ducked, but I suppose it took a second for my brain to work it out. It was just so..." I shrugged. "I couldn't quite believe it. Anyway, I heard the whine again and more bark splintered. That got me moving. I went around to the other side of the tree. That's when Paul saw me and came over with the umbrella."

"You mentioned earlier that you looked toward the hedge," Quimby said, his voice calm and reasonable with none of the slightly accusatory overtones he'd used yesterday when he asked about the length of Alex's phone call.

"Yes, that's right. I looked around the tree, but didn't see anyone."

He tapped away on his phone, then said, "Did you happen to mention to anyone that you saw Ms. Brown on the path behind your cottage?"

"No—well—I didn't tell anyone, but Melissa told me she'd heard about it from Felix."

Quimby's face tightened as he flicked his finger across the screen on his phone. "That would be Melissa Millbank and Felix Carrick?"

"Yes," I said, wondering if I'd have any friends left in the production before the day was out.

Quimby put his phone away and stood.

I pushed back my chair. "Are we done? Can I get back to work…well, at least see if there's anything left for me to do?"

"Yes, except for one thing. Ms. Sharp, I tried to warn you about being careful…"

"What did I do? I was working—doing my job. How was I supposed to know that someone would shoot at me?"

Quimby sighed. "Yes. Well. That is true. All the same, again, please be circumspect in what you say."

I bristled. "I didn't say anything. When I got here, the word was already out. People were talking about Alex being a suspect, and the fact that I'd seen the woman who died."

"Yes," Quimby said grimly, and then under his breath, he added, "Village inquiries have their own challenges."

The back door to the kitchen flew open, and Alex came in. "Kate," he said as he spotted me and came directly over. "Are you okay?"

I thought he was about to embrace me, but he stopped and lightly held my shoulders, his gaze searching my face.

"I'm fine. Everything is okay." He was close enough that I could see the rain weighing down his hair. I'm not normally a close-quarters kind of person, but I didn't have any desire to step back from Alex.

"Mr. Norcutt, I have a few questions for you."

"Of course you do." Alex didn't look away from me, and I found his dark brown gaze sort of mesmerizing. I couldn't have looked away if I'd wanted to.

"I'm fine. Really," I said.

"You're sure?"

"Yes."

Alex ran his hands lightly up and down my arms, then released me. I swallowed and went to get my raincoat off the back of the chair with trembling fingers. Who knew that such a light touch could move me so much? I whipped the coat on and caught Quimby frowning, his gaze shifting between us.

I looked back at Alex. "I'll wait for you out front."

"There's no need for that." Alex pulled a chair out and gestured for me to have a seat. "Why don't you stay."

"Are you sure you want Ms. Sharp here?" Quimby asked.

"Yes. I have nothing to hide."

"All right then." Quimby waved his hand, and we all took a seat, Alex and me on one side of the table and Quimby on the other.

"What have you done today, Mr. Norcutt?"

"I dropped Kate here at six then went on to Parkview Hall to oversee the tear down there."

"And how long were you there?"

"All day. I got the call about what had happened on my way back here."

"Who called you?"

"Melissa Millbank."

I looked down at the table, thinking that despite Melissa's flighty appearance, she was very astute.

"So you were in your car?"

Alex nodded. "Right." As Alex spoke, he kept glancing over at me.

"Did anyone see you leave Parkview Hall?"

"Yes. Beatrice, Lady Stone, walked out with me."

"And what time was this?"

At that question, Alex shifted his full attention to Quimby and said guardedly, "Around two. We finished up quite a bit earlier than I expected."

I suppressed a groan as Quimby said with exact diction, "I see."

Alex's glance flew to me and then back to Quimby. "Don't tell me that's when this…shooting…happened."

Quimby didn't say anything, and Alex looked back to me. "Afraid so."

Alex's eyes widened. "I can't believe it."

Quimby said as his phone buzzed, "Yes, rather odd, that." He read a message which sent his eyebrows toward his hairline. He tapped out a reply, then carefully set the phone down on the table and fixed his gaze on Alex. "Amy Brown's car has been found." Quimby waited a moment and studied Alex's face as if looking for a certain reaction. "Here in Nether Woodsmoor."

My gaze was zipping from Quimby to Alex, who looked wary. "Where?" Alex asked.

"You don't know?"

Alex's voice went low. "No, I don't know. I told you. I didn't know her. How could I know where her car was?" Frustration and a touch of anger laced his words.

Quimby said, "Amy Brown's car was found in the small car park at the bike trail that goes from here to," he paused to consult his text message, but Alex sagged just a bit, and I knew that he'd already guessed which bike trail Quimby would name, as I had. "Here it is. Upper Benning." Quimby put his phone down, clasped his hands, and leaned forward over the table. "The local constable informs me that it is quite easy to get from the car park to the path behind Cottage Lane. Just a short walk."

"Yes. I've walked it many times," Alex said, his voice clipped.

"The gray car." I shifted toward Alex and gripped his arm. "I saw it yesterday when I walked down to the store." When I was in the church hall, I'd heard Quimby and the other investigator describing Amy Brown's car, but I hadn't made the connection.

Alex waved a hand. "See. There you go. Probably everyone who lives on Cottage Lane cuts through there sometime."

"Hmm…possibly. But you were there recently. In fact, you parked there the day Amy Brown died. It's in your statement as well as Ms. Sharp's." Quimby's gaze shifted to me for a moment.

I crossed my arms and sat back. "We weren't looking at cars in the parking area," I said. "We had been blocked from going down our street because of a fire. We wanted to get back to our homes. I didn't pay any attention to the other cars in the parking area."

Quimby shifted his attention back to Alex. "But perhaps Mr. Norcutt did." Quimby leaned farther over the table. "You saw the car, knew it belonged to Amy Brown. She was in the bike race, which you'd both participated in a few days earlier. Perhaps you…connected with Amy then, but now that Ms. Sharp is here…well, maybe you didn't like it that Amy had returned to Nether Woodsmoor."

"And I murdered her?" Alex said, incredulously. "No. If your little story that you've made up were true…if I'd met her at the bike race, and she returned but I didn't want her here, I'd just talk to her." Alex had been speaking quickly, but now he slowed down. "But it doesn't matter because I didn't meet her at the bike race. I didn't know her." He said the last sentence, slowly, spacing out each word. He stood, shoving his chair back roughly. "I thought honesty was the way to go here. I've laid out what I know—very little—but since you insist on seeing everything in the worst possible light and fabricating motives out of thin air, I won't speak to you again without an attorney."

Alex stalked out of the kitchen, right into the pouring rain. I stood and carefully pushed both chairs under the table. "If he hurt that woman—Amy Brown—because of me, then why would he shoot at me? That's what you're implying. You can't have it both ways—that he killed her to be with me and then turned around and tried to kill me. It doesn't make any sense."

"It does if you're the person who can link him to Amy Brown. You saw them together."

"I didn't see them together. I saw her walking behind him. I never said they talked or even acknowledged each other."

"But you didn't stay to watch what happened," Quimby said flatly.

"You can't really think Alex had something to do with Amy Brown's death."

"It's the direction the evidence is pointing, Ms. Sharp. I just follow the evidence."

CHAPTER 12

I TOSSED UP THE HOOD of my raincoat and sprinted for Alex's MG, catching up to him and sliding into the passenger seat seconds after Alex closed his door. The rain drummed against the soft top of the convertible.

Alex shot me a surprised glance. "Are you sure you want to ride with me? There are still a few folks around. I'm sure one of them can give you a ride."

Almost everyone had cleared out, but I had spotted the parking manager collecting cones, and Jeff stood beside a constable in the shelter of the alcove of Coventry House's front door.

"Don't think you'll get out of giving me a ride so easily. Of course, I'm riding with you."

Alex smiled weakly. "I understand if you don't want to, Kate. Quimby thinks I murdered...good grief, I can't even remember her name," Alex said with a bitter laugh. "Too bad Quimby isn't here to witness it. Of course, he'd just assume that I had a one-night stand with her and wanted to get her out of my hair now that you've shown up."

"Alex, don't." I shifted sideways to face him, pressing my

shoulder into the seat. "I don't think you had anything to do with Amy Brown's death. You're the only suspect he has. That's the reason he's focused on you."

"Right. Amy Brown. It's such a forgettable name." He rubbed his forehead. "But it won't be long before he shows up at my door with search warrants, looking for her DNA or something that will link me to her."

"But he's not going to find anything."

"No," Alex said, but in a tone that indicated it wouldn't matter. Alex started the car and drove slowly down the drive and through the gates. Once back on the road, he turned the wipers to high, picked up speed, and we both fell silent. I was sure Alex was preoccupied with his conversation with Quimby, but I was thinking more about why someone would want to shoot at me. Had I just been an easy target in my yellow raincoat for some mentally unhinged person who'd decided today was the day to take a few potshots at a random person?

"Kate."

"What? Oh, sorry," I said, realizing the car was stopped directly by the front gate to my cottage. "Lost in my own thoughts."

"What were you shaking your head about?" Alex asked.

"I don't understand why someone would shoot at me. I was trying to work out if it could be some random crazy person, but I don't think so."

Alex dropped his hand from the wheel. "I'm a jerk. That—discussion—I had with Quimby completely wiped everything else out of my mind. Are you really okay?"

I shrugged one shoulder. "Yeah. I mean, I feel a little skittish." I glanced around, taking in the dark trees bunched at the end of the lane. "I want to think it was a mistake, but that's not likely is it?" I rushed on before he could reply. "But then if it was on purpose, and Quimby seemed to think it was, why would someone shoot at *me*?" I pushed Quimby's explanation out of my mind. Alex wouldn't kill Amy Brown in the first place, so I couldn't be a threat to him.

"I don't know."

"Am I a threat to someone?" I asked. "Do I know something... did I see something that I haven't realized? But that can't be what happened because I certainly didn't see the murderer. You and Amy Brown were the only people on the path. I don't know any more who murdered Amy Brown than...than...DCI Quimby."

"You're absolutely sure you didn't see anyone else on the path that day besides me and this Amy Brown?"

"No. There was no one else." I settled my tote bag on my shoulder as I prepared to step out of the car. "Maybe it was to scare me, but again...why? If I didn't see anything, why frighten me? Unless of course it's someone who doesn't like Americans and just wants me to leave. Oh, wait, I think I just described Elise."

Alex turned the car off and pocketed his keys. "That would be going a little far, even for her. I'll come in and take a look around for you, make sure everything is okay."

"Oh, you don't have to do that."

"Kate, someone shot at you today. I'm not going to drop you off at an empty house and drive away casually."

"Well, when you put it like that..."

The rain pummeled us as we came up the path, and we were soaked by the time I got the sticky door lock open. We fell into the entry, cascades of water dripping off our coats and shoes.

"I'll try not to make any more of a mess," Alex said, gesturing to the puddles of water. He hooked his waterproof jacket on the door handle, then worked off his shoes and left them by the door. "I'll just have a quick look around."

I hung my jacket on a hook by the door and wiped my damp hands on the back of my jeans.

Alex looked around the front room. "Intriguing choice of décor."

"It's a great conversation starter, I'm discovering."

"I can see how it would be. I assume you're going for irony. Utilitarian furniture contrasted with the excessively cozy surroundings to make a point."

"What, you don't like it?"

"Err—actually…"

I laughed. "I'm not nearly so deep. Leftovers from the prior tenant."

"Ah. I see. Yeah, it's not really your style," he said as he checked in the kitchen then took the steps two at a time to the loft.

"No," I agreed, trying to remember how messy I'd left the bedroom. Had I made the bed? Left various bits of clothing strung around the room? I was normally a very neat and exact person, but at five in the morning in a different time zone those little habits tend to drop away. I really couldn't recall what state it was in. I'd barely managed to drag myself from the bed to the shower.

He was back down the stairs before I'd moved away from the front door. "Quick check here." He opened the door to the storage area under the stairs. "Looks good." He passed me, returning to the front door, where he worked his feet into his shoes and shrugged into his jacket. "All clear."

"Thanks."

"No problem." He opened the door, then paused and turned back, his hand still on the latch. "Kate, I really appreciate your… support, I guess. Thanks for not believing the worst about me."

"How could I believe the worst about you? You're thoughtful and kind and you really listen when I talk." I could tell he was about to wave my words away, but I caught his arm. "No, don't shrug it off. You're a good friend. You basically got me the job here—"

"Which I think you're having serious second thoughts about," he inserted, a grin quirking up the corner of his mouth.

"Elise has given me pause, I will admit that. But I'm not sorry I came. Besides, you stood by me when things got a little," I waggled my head, "troublesome, shall we say. You didn't leave me to sort things out on my own last month. You carted me around the countryside and were as invested in finding the truth as I was." I realized what a serious speech that was, so I added. "And you bring me coffee. All the time, which I really appreciate."

The small smile on Alex's face had grown as I spoke. Suddenly he leaned forward and brushed his lips against mine. I froze at the delicate touch, immobilized, my mind jumping through impressions—his warm lips, the rough fabric of his jacket under my hand, the rain gurgling loudly along the drain outside.

He pulled back a millimeter. "Not just friends, I hope."

"No," I managed to whisper back. Somehow the single word came out rough and breathless.

"Good." He brushed his lips over mine again, more slowly this time then pulled me close. I melted into him.

After a while he stepped back.

"Kate. I—" he stopped and spoke under his breath. "Now is definitely not the time."

"What? Now's not the time for what?"

"There's something I have to tell you, but I have to sort out this mess with Quimby first."

"Okay," I said a little uncertainly. "We can talk now…"

"No, I can't stay," he said, and I saw that his breathing was as unsteady as mine. "See you tomorrow, Kate." He smiled at me before pulling the door open and racing down the steps through the rain.

I stood there a moment, watching him, not even caring that I was standing in a puddle of water and my socks were getting soaked.

~

A KNOCK SOUNDED, and I hurried down the stairs. I had mopped up the puddles near the front door and changed into dry socks, all in a happy haze brought on by that kiss. I shoved the lock open, slid the bolt back, and threw the door wide. Elise stood on the doorstep holding a humongous black umbrella over her head. A blue sedan with dark tinted windows idled on the lane. The day was already overcast, and her umbrella blocked out most of the gloomy ambient light, casting her face into shadow. With only her chin and pale pinched lips in view, there was a definite resemblance to the Grim Reaper.

"Oh." I felt my face rearrange itself from an open smile to something more businesslike. "Elise. Would you like to come—"

"No. I can't stay, but I felt I should come in person to make sure there was no misunderstanding."

An ominous beginning, very suitable for her harvester of death look. I managed to keep these thoughts to myself. "How can I help you?"

She tilted the umbrella back, and I could see her whole face now, clenched jaw, angry eyes and all. "You're fired. Do not return to any filming location. If you do, I will have you forcibly removed."

For a moment, Elise's voice faded. Her lips moved, but like that moment during takeoff when you are climbing and your ears go stuffy, I couldn't hear her. *This can't be happening. I've never been fired in my life. I'm a hard worker. My bosses love me.* Even at the temporary jobs I'd held while trying to get back on my feet after I had to quit grad school, my bosses had never had one complaint. Then my ears seemed to pop, and sound rushed back in.

"...hired you on Alex's recommendation, but you've put the cast and crew—the whole production, really—at risk. I can't have that. I'm sure you understand."

"No, I don't. What happened today was not my fault."

"Wasn't it?"

"No," I said, incredulously. "How could it be my fault?"

She blew out a breath through her nose. "You're American." Even speaking the word seemed to pain her. "Your country has that strange fascination with guns."

"But *I* didn't shoot anyone."

"Nevertheless, I have made my decision. Mary will see that you receive payment for the days you...worked, if we can call it that. I imagine you spent most of them mooning around after Alex."

I felt as if I'd been punched in the gut. The unfairness of her accusations...sure I was interested in Alex and there was something between us, but we'd done our jobs. "That's unfair. Alex and I have always behaved in an appropriate manner." Thoughts of the kiss rushed into my mind, and I felt my cheeks heat. "On the set," I added quickly, then raised my chin. What was wrong with me? Romance on a film set wasn't forbidden. It was common, practically a rule. If there *wasn't* flirting and romance, then that would be weird.

Elise ignored me, her gaze ranging over the exterior of the cottage. "I understand we're also paying for your lodging because there was some sort of snafu at the inn," she said in a tone that indicated she thought I'd fabricated the broken pipe at the inn. Her attention snapped back to me. "Your cushy ride is over. The production won't pick up another day of this rental."

She whirled away and went down the steps. I raced after her, splashing through the path, my socks absorbing the water. I gripped her shoulder. "Wait."

She shied back from me, and I quickly pulled my hand away. At the rate she was going, she'd have the constable here in moments and accuse me of assault.

"Why do you hate me?"

"I don't hate you," she said, her words automatic.

"Yes, you do. You really do. Why? Sure, the production had to close down early today, and I'm sorry that happened, but if you look at it objectively, you have to admit that I didn't cause that. I was the victim in that situation. This is about something else. From the moment we met, it's been clear you can't stand me." I felt the rain soaking into my hair, plastering it to my forehead and pressing my shirt to my shoulders and back, but I waited.

The raindrops thumped onto her umbrella in the silence, then she drew in a breath. "People should rise on their own merit," she said tightly.

"I agree," I said, puzzled.

Elise let out a snort. "That is quite rich, coming from you." She turned and stalked away.

I dodged around her and gripped the gate. I held it closed, blocking her path. "What in the world are you talking about?"

She gave an impatient shake of her head. "Women like you make me sick. I've worked hard to get where I am. Do you know what I had to put up with when I was your age? How many groping hands I had to fight off? How much harder I had to work than the men who were my contemporaries? I wasn't part of the old boys' club. I had to fight and work doubly hard to get where I am today. Women like you, who use your looks and your youth to rise through the ranks, disgust me. We needed an additional location scout and manager, so I hired you, but that was before I heard how close you were to your old boss, how you raced out here at the first sign of trouble for him. And now you're cozying up to Alex. I hope he knows what he's getting himself into."

She pushed by me, whipped through the gate, and got in the car. I was so stunned that I didn't move. The gate fell back and hit me on the hip as the car accelerated away.

I turned and slowly went back to the cottage. I felt as if I'd just experienced one of those jolting earthquakes that sometimes rocked through California, jiggling the earth and making me reach out blindly for something solid to hang on to. I squished inside the cottage and leaned against the door, water streaming off me. "Well, my life is in shambles," I muttered.

~

BY THE TIME I'd showered, changed, and cleaned up the floor *again*, I'd moved from shock and denial into anger that focused my attention. Elise was wrong. Completely wrong. She didn't know me, but she'd made up her mind about me. I couldn't do anything about that. So, first order of business was a job.

I had to work. During the last few years, I'd focused on helping my mom get on her feet after the divorce and paying off student loan debt from my short-lived time as a grad student. As a result, my saving account balance was low—and that was looking at it optimistically. I had used a large part of my savings to purchase my airline ticket, thinking that I'd make it back up working on the documentary, but I'd probably only earned enough during the last few days to purchase a meal in coach on my return flight.

I sent a text to Marci, my old office manager, telling her things had changed and asked her if she knew of anyone looking for a location scout. She texted back immediately. *In meeting. Will call later. Leon asked about you?!? Will shake the trees, see what I hear.*

"Eww." I cringed. Leon Bettis with his groping hands and roving gaze was exactly the sort of guy Elise had described earlier. Working for Leon was dead last on my list. I would be willing to do quite a few other jobs so that I didn't have to work for him, despite his status as Hollywood's up-and-coming location manager.

I plopped down on the uncomfortable couch and settled my laptop on my crossed legs. My search for flights revealed that the first flight that I could afford to L.A. left next week. It was a non-returnable fare. The difference between the airfare leaving within the next day or so and the one next week was significant. The fare next week would still take a huge chunk out of my available credit on my credit card, but I could swing it. Probably. If I got home and got some work, even some freelance stuff lined up quickly. I would actually save quite a bit of money by staying in England for a few more days. Maybe I could work a deal with Beatrice to do some sideline photography work for her in exchange for staying in the cottage for a few more days. I'd become fairly handy with the camera in the last few years. Maybe Parkview Hall needed a few beauty shots for brochures or for their website. Even if that didn't work out, I'd still be better off leaving next week. The difference between the ticket prices was that large.

I hovered the curser over the purchase button, going back and forth over what was best. I needed to work. No, correction. I *had* to work. The odds of me stumbling into another location scouting job here in England were slim, especially if Elise spoke to anyone else about me. My best odds of getting work were in the States, but that kiss…it had been quite a kiss. Full of potential.

That Louis Armstrong song, *A Kiss to Build A Dream On*, flitted through my mind. At the dentist's office where I'd put in so many of my hours at my temp job, we'd had a heavy rotation of Big Band, Swing, and early Rock and Roll pumped through the office sound system. I circled the cursor on the screen, which made the BOOK SEATS button highlight and fade.

If I went back to California, things between us could still develop, but beginning a relationship on different continents just didn't seem the best way to start things off. And I did want to give it a go with Alex. I really did. Despite Quimby's warnings and the mess Alex was mixed up in right now. He was genuine and sweet and he made me laugh. The first two qualities were hard to find, but of all the guys I'd dated recently, I couldn't think of one who made me laugh.

I looked away from the laptop screen to the front window. Tulips were pushing up through the earth, and a branch of one of the rosebushes bent toward the ground, each tightly furled flower bud, dripping with rain. The pile of burnt debris from Lilac Cottage, now soaked and soggy, still sat at the curb.

Everything hinged on Quimby's investigation. I was pretty sure how Alex felt about me—that kiss had left little room for doubt—but until the death of Amy Brown was sorted out, we'd be entangled in that. Quimby's ever-closing circle around Alex meant that Alex had to focus on that, not on what was happening or what might happen between us. Being a murder suspect meant that everything else slipped right down to the bottom of the priority list.

Okay, then. In for a penny, in for a pound, I thought as I minimized the flight search. I'd spend the next day, doing everything and anything I could to help Alex clear his name. He had helped me when things got rough. I would do my best to return the favor. If I'd made no progress, I'd book the ticket tomorrow. Hopefully, the price wouldn't go up in the next twenty-four hours. I resolutely pushed away the surge of anxiety that thought brought on and opened a new window on the laptop, determined to figure out what connection Amy Brown had with Nether Woodsmoor that didn't involve Alex.

CHAPTER 13

*W*HAT WAS THAT AWFUL THUMPING noise? I struggled out of a deep sleep and shifted from my back to my side, then reflexively put out a hand to grab my laptop as I felt it shift and begin to slide off my stomach. I wiggled up onto my elbow and looked around. I'd stretched out and fallen asleep on the couch. My Moleskine notebook sat on the floor beside a plate with crumbs from my hasty sandwich dinner. I'd closed the curtains when the sun went down last night, and they were still closed against the darkness now. I checked my watch. Five-thirty a.m.

I recalled fighting off yawns as I made notes while searching various social media for Amy Brown, a nearly endless task, and thinking I really should go to bed, but Amy Brown was extremely active on social media and the information available on the web is endless. The constant loading of prior status updates, old posts, and ancient tweets had lured me on until well after midnight.

The pounding noise came again. "Kate, are you in there?" The heavy door muffled Alex's voice, but I could still hear the edge of worry in his words.

I stood, pushing my twisted and matted hair out of my eyes as

I went to the door and wrenched it open. A faint glow from the horizon silhouetted Alex and Slink as they stood on the step. Alex had on a T-shirt, shorts, and running shoes. His hair was plastered to his forehead, and his shirt was stained with sweaty patches. Slink's sides were heaving, and her tongue lolled out of the side of her mouth. Between breaths, Alex said, "Kate. I was worried. You didn't answer your phone."

I patted my pockets. I usually had my phone somewhere on my person, but I didn't have it with me at the moment. "Sorry. Um…" I looked around and spotted my tote bag on a chair in the front room. "It's probably buried in my bag, still on vibrate."

"No, that's fine. I was just worried. You know, with everything that's happened." He reached up and used the back of his arm to wipe his forehead. "I took Slink for a quick run before I have to leave." At her name, Slink looked up at him with adoring eyes.

Normally, sweaty guys were a major turn off, but there was something about the way his shirt clung to his chest and abs as his muscles flexed with his movements that made me completely lose my train of thought. I brought my gaze up to his face. It was hard to tell with the light behind him, but I was almost sure his eyes were twinkling at me.

I cleared my throat. "Right. Yes. Thank you for checking on me. Doing fine." I gestured toward the couch, then became aware that my shirt was bunched up and twisted halfway around my waist. I pulled it straight. "I fell asleep, doing a bit of research."

"Well, you better get moving. We need to leave in fifteen. Can you make it? Wait, of course you can. I remember how fast you got changed that day we met." He was backpedaling, moving down the steps to the path as he spoke, letting Slink's leash out. "I better hurry or you'll beat me."

"No. I can't."

He checked his watch. "Well, we can do twenty, but that's pushing it. After yesterday, we have a lot to do."

"No, I mean I can't go with you." I stepped onto the porch. "Elise fired me yesterday."

He stared at me a moment, his forehead wrinkled like I'd spoken in a foreign language. "But she can't do that. We need you."

"Apparently not. Or at least, Elise thinks you can do fine without me. I put the cast and crew as well as the production at risk."

"That's insane."

I leaned against the doorframe. "Between you and me, she doesn't like me. She was looking for a reason to fire me. Getting shot at was the perfect excuse."

"But that's not right. You were the victim."

"She doesn't see it that way."

"Well, if you go. I go."

I closed my eyes briefly. "I appreciate that, but you need the job, right?"

"Only if I want to pay my bills."

"I thought so. Stay with the production. Don't make an enemy of Elise. She has clout, doesn't she? She could make your life miserable, if she wanted to."

"Yes."

"So don't get on her bad side by taking mine. Go to work. I can go back to the States, find something there, if I have to."

Alex wound the leash around his palm. "What about..."

"Yesterday afternoon?" I couldn't help but smile at him as I motioned back and forth between us. "That thing?"

He smiled back. "Yes, that thing. Personally, I enjoyed it and would like to pursue more of it...see where it goes."

"Me, too. I don't want to leave, but I may have to. I have bills to pay, too. But it won't be for a few days, at least. In the meantime, I'm focusing on what I can do here to help you get Quimby off your back."

Alex narrowed his eyes at me. "How do you intend to do that?"

"I'm going through all of Amy Brown's social media accounts." Alex looked relieved. "She's got to have some connection with Nether Woodsmoor besides you," I said. "People post a scary amount of information online. Some little tidbit might be the thing that gives Quimby a new trail to follow."

"Don't you think the police are doing that?"

"I'm sure it's on their list, but it's more than likely that they're looking to see how she was connected to you." His faced changed. The light seemed to seep out of him. "Sorry," I said.

"Don't be. It's probably a very good assessment of the situation."

"But we both know those inquiries will be a dead end. No, I'm looking for a connection to Rafe. It makes the most sense. She was found in his cottage, after all."

Alex crossed his arms and leaned against the handrail attached to the steps. "But then why leave her there to be discovered in the fire? That's pretty stupid. He had to know her body would be found."

"But the fire was an accident. He had no idea firefighters would be tramping through his cottage. He left her there and went out to establish an alibi."

"But I thought he had a solid alibi."

"But how closely has Quimby checked it? Is it really possible that the librarians had an eye on him every minute of that afternoon? Couldn't he have slipped out and back in? Is there a back door to the library? Or is there one to the pub?"

"I don't know."

"See," I said triumphantly. "All good questions that I'm sure Quimby hasn't pursued because he's been so focused on you. All I need is something that ties Amy Brown to Rafe Farraday. That will force Quimby to look into him more deeply."

"I'm not convinced that is what would happen, but as long as you're staying online and not accusing Rafe to his face, I'll stay out of your way."

I flared an eyebrow. "That's good because I'm doing it whether or not you approve."

"Yeah. I thought you'd say that." He looked at his watch again. "Okay. You do...your research thing. I'll go to work, but with the goal of getting you hired back."

"I think that's a long shot."

"I'll take my chances."

I WAS CRUNCHING my way through a bowl of cereal when there was another knock on the door. Good grief, couldn't a girl have breakfast and a shower before being flooded with callers? Alex should be long gone by now. If he was knocking on my door instead of overseeing setup at this moment, Elise would probably fire him, too.

Still holding my cereal bowl, I padded over to the front door. "Who's there?" I had opened the door earlier because I recognized Alex's voice, but I wasn't about to unbolt it, not with everything that had happened over the last few days.

"Hey, Kate. It's me, Melissa."

Melissa? I muttered and slid back the bolt. "Hey," I said as I opened the door.

"I came by to see if you're okay."

"There seems to be a lot of that going around. I'm fine. What brought this on?" Was everyone concerned with my well-being this morning? I mean, it was nice that people were worried about me, but I didn't really want a ton of visitors dropping in on me all day.

"I got a text from Mary that said you were banned from the production and no one should have any contact with you."

"So you ran right over?"

"Yeah." She grinned. "That's me, a rebel at heart."

"Well, as you can see, I'm fine. Scruffy, but fine. Haven't showered yet. You, on the other hand, look amazing. Want some coffee?" She'd gone from sweatshirt and jeans to the other end of the fashion spectrum with a white ruffled poet shirt, black slacks, and a pair of black stilettos. Her bangs were still fuchsia, but she'd brushed them to the side and tucked the rest of her blond hair back behind her ears.

"Sure." She followed me to the kitchen and accepted a mug of coffee.

"I'm beginning to wonder about Mary. Does she really exist? I've never seen her, and now I guess I never will."

"Oh, she exists, but she's not here. She's a virtual assistant. She lives somewhere in America. New Jersey? New Mexico? Somewhere new, anyway."

I put my cereal bowl in the sink, topped off my mug, and waved her to the table. "Got a job interview today?"

"No." Her lace-trimmed sleeve flared and expanded as she brought her mug to her lips. "I like to mix it up. Keep things fresh. I'd get bored if I wore the same stuff every day."

I glanced down at my fitted white oxford shirt and jeans. "Not like me," I said, thinking of my similar shirts in different hues hanging on the tiny closet rod upstairs. I had to admit that my wardrobe was pretty tame, compared to Melissa. Every once in a while, I changed things up with a linen tank or a casual long-sleeved knit shirt, but I certainly didn't own a poet shirt or anything with fringe. "Sometimes I go crazy and wear stripes."

Melissa put down her mug. "You look great. You've got that classic, elegant style. Basic colors, clean lines. It suits you. Don't get me started on fashion. I could natter on about it all day, but I can't—"

"Because you have a job to get to," I finished for her. "Don't worry. It's okay. I'm not about to dissolve into tears because Elise fired me. I'm working on something else, a side project."

"Good. I'll let you know if I hear of anyone looking for a location scout."

"Thanks. I appreciate that."

"Sure." She took a last sip of her coffee and stood to put it in the sink. "We never did meet for that drink. We should do that, but I can't tonight. I'm meeting Bill."

"Who's Bill?"

"The hot policeman."

"Detective Sergeant Olney? Wow. What happened with the computer guy? Hector?"

"I tried to chat him up at the pub the other night, and he was definitely not interested. Must be gay," she said with a shrug. "Anyway, how about that drink? Maybe tomorrow at the pub, or do you want to come to thrilling Upper Benning?"

"The pub would be great. And I should still be here."

"What?"

"I may have to go back to California. Got to work, you know."

"Hmm. Alex will be disappointed."

"Yeah, me too. It's not like I want to go."

"Well, maybe Elise will change her mind and hire you back."

"You've worked with her before?" I asked.

"Yes, on loads of projects."

"Has she ever done that, hired someone back?"

Melissa contemplated the ceiling for a moment. "No, never."

"I better start working my contact list."

"Good idea."

CHAPTER 14

FTER SHOWERING, I SPENT HALF the morning networking, searching for job openings or freelance work, then went back to searching Amy Brown's social media. At eleven, I slapped my laptop closed and rotated my shoulders. I had nothing. Absolutely nothing. Amy Brown had no personal connections in Nether Woodsmoor. Sure, she came for the bike race, but that was the only mention of the village that I could find.

I now knew she was sporty and enjoyed biking, swimming, and running. She liked pictures of cats, both cute and grumpy versions, took lots of selfies to show off her outfits, and had a passion for nail art—painting her fingernails with different colors or patterns to match what she was wearing or the season.

I had wondered if what drew her to Nether Woodsmoor was a connection to Rafe Farraday or the Jane Austen letters—if she'd somehow discovered their existence, but as far as I could tell from the information she listed on social media, she didn't have a special interest in English literature or any sort of advanced degree. I couldn't find a mention of Rafe Farraday. I suppose that she could have been a student in his online class, but she never mentioned books at all, much less Jane Austen, *Pride and Prejudice*, Mr. Darcy, or even Colin Firth.

She listed a software company as her employer and her job title as social marketing specialist, but her posts from a few years ago about working the receptionist desk made it clear that she'd worked her way up to her current position.

Before I'd dipped into her online life, she'd simply been a name, but now I was getting to know her, and the more I read about her, the sadder it made me.

I slipped on my wedges and grabbed a black cardigan to go over my tank. Perhaps I needed to approach the problem from a different angle. Instead of digging into Amy Brown's life and looking for a connection between her and Rafe, maybe the quickest way to turn the investigation away from Alex would be to focus on poking a few holes in Rafe's alibi.

It didn't look like rain, but I brought an umbrella with me anyway. It was England in the spring, after all. It was a beautiful, clear day with a hint of a breeze. I was spooked after yesterday's events and glanced up and down Cottage Lane before stepping outside. Everything looked completely normal, idyllic even.

A woman was walking her dog, a corgi, along the lane, and down in the village, I could see a few cars moving along beside people walking into the shops. I swallowed and stepped outside, falling in a few paces behind the dog walker. I wasn't going to stay holed up in my cottage out of fear of what might happen. If I lived that way, I might as well ask Quimby for a police escort to the airport and fly home now. Besides, I'd been alone in a deserted part of the grounds on Coventry House when the person had shot at me. I intended to stay within the village and always have someone around me.

As I paced down the street and heard nothing except a few birds calling, I relaxed. The heavy rains must have been exactly what the gardens needed. Flowers in all shades expanded in the sunlight, creating bursts of color everywhere from the small cottage gardens to the window boxes along the high street. I passed the pub and went on until I reached the village library. The local newspaper didn't have a searchable online database of articles, and I hoped the library would have back issues with more detailed news about the fire.

I was the only patron in sight and went directly to the desk where a young woman looked up from stacking books on a cart. She was probably in her early twenties, had curly blond hair, an open, eager face, and a nametag reading CHRISTINA pinned to her short-sleeved sweater. Just the person I was looking for.

"Can I help you?" she asked.

"Hi, I'm looking for copies of your local paper," I said, deciding to start with the research request before branching out into testing the solidity of Rafe's alibi.

"The *Nether Woodsmoor Advisor,* you mean?"

"Yes, that's the one."

"Current issues or past?"

"The last week or so."

She took me to a section of shelves positioned around two upholstered chairs. "Here you are." She pointed to a thin stack of newsprint. "I can help you find older issues, if you like."

I flicked through the stack, which contained a month's worth of issues. "No, that won't be necessary." My big city-ness was showing. I'd forgotten how small Nether Woodsmoor was. Their paper was a weekly. The most current issue had come out the day before the fire, so I was out of luck there. And it looked as if most of the stories dealt with community events instead of hard news. I replaced the stack on the shelf. "I was looking for news about the fire, something with a local angle."

"We don't have anything like that. The local paper is more a listing of events, things for sale, advertisements, that sort of thing. And we're not big enough to make the news in the larger cities." She crossed her arms and leaned a hip against one of the chairs. "So sad about the fire."

"Yes, it was. I heard the man whose cottage burned was here the afternoon it happened."

"Oh, he was. Came in to research his book. We didn't have quite the range of materials he was looking for, but I was able to find him several books on Austen. So popular, Jane is."

"So you were here that day and saw him?"

"Of course. We're only open four days a week, so anytime we're open, I'm here."

"And he was here all afternoon?"

"Yes."

"He didn't slip out to get a coffee or go for a quick walk?"

"No." She pointed to a row of tables near the non-fiction section. "He sat right there the whole time."

"I see. Thanks for your help." I moved to the door, scanning the room. There was no back exit, and the restroom was near the front door, which was in direct sight of the checkout desk. The whole area was so small that even if Christina had been shelving books in another corner of the library she would still be able to see the tables and the front door. Rafe couldn't have slipped out without her noticing, if she was telling the truth, and her helpful, anxious to please face looked so guileless that I thought she was being honest with me.

"I'd hoped he would come again. He had so many questions and needed so much help that day that I was sure he'd be back," she said almost wistfully. Library patronage was clearly on the low side, but I figured Rafe's handsomeness probably had something to do with her hope he would return.

"So he hasn't come back?"

"No. That was the one and only time he's been in." We reached the checkout desk. She plucked a brochure from a display. "Would you like a library card? We have a nice selection of popular fiction. Plenty of genres to choose from. Or, if you're a non-fiction type, we have lots of guides to the area. Country walks, history of the region. It won't take but a minute," she said. "There's no wait."

"Normally, yes, I'd get one. I love Jane Austen, but I may not be in town much longer."

She sighed. "We get that a lot. People just in for the day or weekend. Well, thanks for stopping in," she said rather forlornly and went back to her rolling cart of books.

I stepped outside the library. The day had been a complete bust as far as helping Alex to clear his name. I should check my email and see if anyone had replied to my messages with job leads. And I ought to look at the airfare again, make sure it hadn't gone up. I had my laptop in my tote bag and could do all that at the pub, which had free Wi-Fi. As I was making my way there, an ancient mud-splattered Range Rover pulled into a parallel parking slot in front of the bakery. Beatrice's faded brunette head emerged, and I darted across the street, calling her name.

"Kate, delightful to see you. Oh, I'm so glad you weren't hurt yesterday. How terribly frightening it must have been."

I should have known Beatrice would know about the shooting yesterday. She kept a close eye on everything in Nether Woodsmoor. "Yes, it was."

"How is the production going?" She asked as she pulled a list from the pocket of her oversized trench coat.

"Progressing without me, I'm sure."

She'd been unfolding the piece of paper, but her hands stilled. "What?"

"Elise fired me. Said I was endangering the production."

"Ridiculous." Beatrice's tone went frosty. "Shall I speak to her on your behalf?"

"No. Please don't. I mean, thank you for the offer, but if she doesn't want me to work for her, I certainly don't want to force myself back in."

"Yes, that would be a recipe for misery."

"I do have a favor to ask." I explained about my situation and tentative plans to fly back to Southern California in a few days, then offered to do some freelance photography in exchange for a few more days in the cottage.

"New professional photos for the website would be just the thing. It's sadly in need of an update—oh, excuse me a moment." She stepped off the sidewalk, directly into the path of a biker, forcing him to stop.

"Mr. Lyons, I've been trying to catch you."

Under the helmet and sunglasses, I recognized Hector. He was fitted out in serious biking gear, spandex shirt and shorts, gloves, and he even had a little mirror attached to his helmet so that he could see behind him. He clicked a button next to a digital readout attached to his handlebars—some kind of sport tracking device, I guessed—and gave Beatrice a minuscule smile. "Lady Stone and er—" he looked toward me. Obviously, he was as bad with names as I was.

"Kate Sharp," I said. "I'm staying in Honeysuckle Cottage."

"Right. Yes."

"Sorry to interrupt your ride, won't take a moment," Beatrice said. "Thank you for participating in the stone wall reconstruction. We so appreciate you taking an interest in the Historical Society. Our next project is an auction to raise funds to reroof the museum, and I think you would make a wonderful master of ceremonies."

It wasn't really a question, more a command actually, but Hector took his time in replying. He flexed his hands, working his gloves down onto his fingers. "No, I couldn't do that. That sort of thing isn't for me. Sorry." He pushed off, neatly gliding by Beatrice. "Got to get on."

She looked after him with a frown. "Hmm. I thought perhaps he was coming out of his shell, but it appears I was wrong. That was the first time he's done anything in the village that wasn't related to biking. So hard to get people interested. I've been trying to get him involved since he moved here a year ago. I guess rebuilding the wall was only an aberration."

"Perhaps he wanted to be involved in it because it was so near his property."

"Yes. Well, I will keep him in mind for any outdoor activities. I'm not giving up on him," Beatrice said. "It's important that newcomers integrate into the community. Otherwise, we'll have two sets of villagers, those that live here year round and those who flit up from London for a holiday weekend, but aren't really invested in the village."

I watched Hector disappear around a corner, his vivid blue shirt making him easily visible even from a distance. I wouldn't want to be on any of Beatrice's lists. I had a feeling once she set her mind to get you involved in something it would probably be easier to just give in and do it rather than fight it.

I made plans to photograph Parkview Hall tomorrow, said good-bye to Beatrice, and went into the pub. It was fairly busy with a lunch crowd, but I snagged one of the tall-backed wooden booths that lined one wall. After a quick trip to the bar to order a plowman's lunch, I returned to the booth and got to work, checking my emails. I had three possibilities, all freelance, one-time gigs, but it was better than nothing. The downside was that they were all in L.A.

I sent off emails inquiring about the work, then checked the airfare and was glad to see it hadn't gone up in price. Louise must have been busy in the kitchen, because another server dropped off my lunch. I pushed my computer away and dug into the meal of ham, cheese, grapes, a chunk of bread, apple slices, and carrots along with some condiments on the side. As I tore off a piece of bread, I heard the words,

"...your publisher will take care of all the traditional review venues."

I leaned to the side and spotted Rafe seated at one of the tables near me. He was turned slightly away, but I could still see his face, and he certainly didn't look like someone who was worried about a murder investigation or even about the loss of the letters. I wondered if Rafe had told Elise about the destruction of the letters yet. He had one hand looped through the handle of a pint as he lounged back in his chair listening to the woman in a black suit who sat across the table from him. Her back was turned to me, so I couldn't see much more than her inky black bob, which was cut to knife-edge sharpness, and the red soles of her incredibly high heels. Becca sat at the table with them, but her attention was fixed on her phone.

The woman with the bob opened a folder and slid it across the table to Rafe as she continued, "This is a sampling of what I've done in the past for other celebrities. We'll use Austen as a hook to draw media interest. Blog posts, newspaper articles, chat shows. We shouldn't have any problem getting attention, not with the material you have. All we have to do is tap into the cult of Austen, and we're golden. Tons of free publicity."

Rafe flicked through the folder and gave a small nod. "Looks good."

"Brilliant," the woman said, reaching for her phone. "Let's talk dates. I envision a two-pronged campaign. Phase one will be associated with the book release, then we can coordinate a second push when the documentary airs. That will give you a nice visibility boost. Now, we'll need to hit media outlets here in the U.K. as well as in the States..."

Rafe closed the folder and pushed it back across the table to her, but she said, "That's for you. Keep it." Rafe leaned over and shoved it into his messenger bag, which was on the floor beside his feet, the flap wrinkled against his leg. He pressed the folder into the bag. As his hand pressed down, I caught a flicker of blue on white in the bag, which for some reason caught my attention. I shifted to the side to see better, but he'd already flung the large flap over the bag, covering its contents.

"What's this I hear about someone firing a gun at you yesterday," Louise asked as she approached my booth, blocking my view of Rafe. "Are you really all right?"

"Yes, fine. No harm done, well, except to my career. Apparently, I'm too dangerous to have around."

Louise frowned her disapproval. "You don't mean..."

"Yes, I'm afraid so. I've been fired. That sounds so awful. Maybe I should say 'let go.' Although, that makes me sound like an animal released into the wild."

Louise pointed her rag at me. "Made redundant. That's the trendy phrase."

"Even worse." Louise looked sympathetic, and I quickly added, "Don't worry. I'll find something else." I motioned to my laptop. "Already on it."

Louise tilted her head as she looked at the screen. "That's the woman who was killed, isn't it?"

"Yes." I must have accidentally brushed my hand across the track pad and reopened one of the windows I'd minimized back at the cottage. Amy Brown's Twitter profile picture smiled out at us from its position beside the banner image she'd chosen, the London skyline.

"The detective had a picture of her, but it didn't look like that." Louise leaned closer to the screen, then she stood up and pressed the fingers of one hand to her lips. "Oh, I was wrong." She started patting her pockets. "Where is that card? I have to call him. Oh—it won't be in this apron. I probably washed it." She tucked her rag into the pocket of her apron and began to untie it. "I'll have to go to the church hall. They're still there, aren't they?"

"Louise, what's wrong?"

"I saw her." She pointed to the laptop. "She was here. That detective chief inspector showed me her picture—a drawing, not a photograph like this—and I said I'd never seen her before, but I was wrong. She was in here. I recognize her now. I didn't in the drawing, but seeing that photo…it was her." She pulled her apron over her head and balled it up, but then stopped. "I can't leave. I'm the only one here until one."

"I have the DCI's number in my phone, or you could call down to the church hall. I'm sure they would send someone up."

"Yes, you're right, of course," she murmured as she shook out her apron.

"So she was here? On the day of the fire?"

"Oh, no. Not that day. The weekend before. Poor girl, I felt sorry for her, having that decrepit Felix bloke trying to buy her drinks and flirt with her."

"Felix? Are you sure?"

"Yes, of course I'm sure. He was too persistent. Couldn't see that she wasn't interested."

"But Melissa said Felix told everyone that he'd seen Alex talking to her."

"Alex? No, Alex didn't go near her. He was here at the same time. We were bursting at the seams after the bike race. Everyone wanted to come in for a pint after it was over. But I never saw Alex talk to her."

"Why would Felix say that?"

"Probably because he didn't want to answer any questions himself." Louise shook her head. "I know his type. I've seen enough to recognize them. Pushy. Won't take no for an answer. I bet there's something in his past—something unsavory. He didn't want the police sniffing around him, so he threw out Alex's name to distract them."

"You think he'd do that?" Mischievousness, I could picture that from Felix, but deliberately throwing suspicion on someone else? I wasn't sure Felix was capable of that, but I didn't really know him well. "So what happened between Felix and Amy Brown?"

"Oh, she set him right. Told him off, she did."

"What was he doing hitting on her? She was at least ten years younger."

"Does that stop a man from trying?" Louise's agitation faded a bit. "Every time he's in here, he's sidling up to some young thing, trying to buy her drinks. Fancies himself a Don Juan, I think, but none of the women ever respond."

Hmm…that would have to hurt after a while. Perhaps he was tired of being rebuffed. He might have seen Amy in the village later and followed her. But even if he did kill her, why would he put her body in Rafe's cottage? Did he even know where Rafe lived? I sighed and went back to my lunch.

Louise went off to call the church hall, and I glanced around the pub. Rafe, Becca, and the woman planning his media assault had cleared out while I was talking to Louise, so I went back to skimming through Amy Brown's online life, but didn't find anything new.

Louise returned later to clear my plate. "It's all settled. I'm to come down to the church hall and give a statement at my convenience. They weren't upset at all."

"Louise, on the day Amy Brown died, you were here?"

"Yes, of course."

"So you saw Rafe?"

"Yes." She lifted my plate in the direction of the bar. "He sat up there, third bar stool from the left the whole evening."

"He never left?"

"No."

"Maybe slipped out the back?"

"No. He was right there in front of me every time I went to get a pint. I would have noticed if he was gone." She looked at me, a frown line appearing between her brows. "What's this? The police asked me these questions and Phil as well," she said, lifting her chin toward the kitchen.

I hadn't met Phil yet; he'd always been in the kitchen whenever I stopped by the pub.

Louise said, "Why are you asking, too?"

I hesitated, debating whether I should tell her anything about the investigation, but Alex had once told me that if there was anyone I could trust in Nether Woodsmoor, it was Louise. She knew how to keep a secret. "Have you got a minute?"

She glanced around the pub. The lunch rush was over and only a few people remained. "Sure." She slid into the booth across from me, putting my plate back down on the table.

I leaned forward and kept my voice low. "Quimby thinks Alex had something to do with Amy Brown's death."

Louise flicked her hand. "Oh, I heard that. Nothing but stuff and rumor."

"No. Alex is a suspect. Quimby has questioned him several times."

"But that's ridiculous," Louise said stoutly.

"I know. I couldn't believe it either, but it's all my fault." I explained how I'd seen them both on the path behind the cottages. "Apparently, Alex was one of the last people to be around her while she was alive. He doesn't even remember seeing her, but since I saw them together..."

Louise patted my hand. "Well, the DCI couldn't very well ignore it. He's got to investigate it."

"Yes, but nothing has turned up to take his attention away from Alex. That's why I was looking at Amy Brown's accounts. I was sure there would be something...some little mention or a photograph or a name that would connect her to someone else here in Nether Woodsmoor. But there's nothing. Maybe the connection is from her childhood or something years ago. If that's the case, then I'm sunk because all of her accounts only go back a few years. It's as if she didn't exist five years ago..."

I sat for a few moments, those words sinking in. Then I pawed through my tote bag and pulled out my Moleskine notebook and flipped back and forth through the notes I'd made. "Yes. That's it."

"Kate, luv, are you feeling okay? You're looking rather flushed."

"That's it. She *didn't* exist five years ago."

CHAPTER 15

"SEE, LOOK." I PUSHED MY notebook across the table and paged backward and forward, tapping the paper. "None of her accounts go back more than three years."

Louise gave me a long look before glancing down at the pages.

"She never mentions a childhood home or anything from the past," I went on. "You know how some people post old pictures of themselves or their family on those days, Throwback Thursdays?"

"No, I don't have much time to play around on the computer."

"Well, some people do. They post pictures from their past on certain days. She never participated."

"Well, maybe she was a private person."

"But she wasn't. Her job was in social media. She posted about the company and software-related issues during her workday and then when she was on her own time, she continued to share…pretty much everything from her day-to-day life—where she went for her bike rides, what clothes she wore, and the food she ate. But now that I think about it, none of the background portions of the sites were filled out. She never listed a hometown or relatives or her schools. And if you're into sharing on social media, why wouldn't you fill out your profiles completely?"

"Maybe she didn't want everyone knowing all those details about her—for security, you know. There's always stories on the telly about identity theft and whatnot."

"I don't think it was to protect her from identity theft. She was too casual about other details that could be used to hack her accounts. She mentioned the name of her bank once when she couldn't get cash from an ATM, and she posted her travel plans before she left as well as pictures when she was gone, which you should never do. It's like posting a neon sign, letting people know you'll be away. No, if she was worried about security she would have been more careful about what she posted."

Louise handed the journal back, still looking doubtful.

"And then there's her name," I continued. "Amy Brown. As Alex said, it's such a forgettable name. So common."

"I don't see what you're getting at." Louise scooted to the end of the booth and picked up the plate. I was vaguely aware that a few people had come into the pub.

"I don't think she was always Amy Brown. For some reason, she changed her name. She didn't want anyone to know about her past—whatever it was—so she went by a different name and never mentioned anything about it online."

Louise still didn't look convinced.

"How do you change your name in England? In the States, I think you have to go to court. Is it like that here?"

"Oh, no. Here you can change it by deed poll."

"Deed poll, what's that?"

Louise looked over her shoulder at a group of bike riders, Hector in the front, moving to the bar, their clips on their shoes making clicking sounds on the hardwood. "It's a form. You fill it out, have someone witness it. My sister did it after her divorce. Just showed it to the bank, and so on, anyone who needed it."

"That seems a little insecure," I said, thinking about terrorists threats that were in the news so often.

Louise shrugged. "That's all it takes. She could have registered it somewhere—I forget where—but I don't think it's required." Louise moved away to serve the customers at the bar. I pulled my computer toward me and typed "deed poll" into the search bar.

A few minutes of searching confirmed what Louise said. You could indeed change your name by deed poll by filling out a form and having it witnessed. Then you simply presented the form to banks and governmental agencies. I dug deeper and found that there was a way to register the name change in a governmental publication, the *Gazette*, which had a webpage. I clicked over to it, entered the name "Amy Brown," and got over four thousand entries. I managed to narrow the results by date then added the qualifier "deed poll," which brought up only two results.

The first one was a woman abandoning the name of Amy Brown to take the name of Amy Blythe. The other was a notice of a woman who abandoned the name of Lillian Helena Stratham to take on the name of Amy Helena Brown. The date on the notice was four years ago. I was reaching for my phone when Louise stopped by my booth again. "Any luck?"

"Yes, I've found a woman named Lillian Helena Stratham who changed her name to Amy Helena Brown four years ago."

Louise looked off into space and repeated the name, then shook her head. "I thought there for a second that it sounded familiar, but I can't place it."

I put my phone down. "Really, it sounded familiar?" Louise nodded, so I did a quick search for the name, but nothing recent came up. "Let's try a few years ago," I said, but Louise had moved away to serve some customers. I set the search to look for information older than three years, and pages and pages of results loaded.

I clicked through to the links. Each one of them were news stories about a financial scam involving a man named Harry

Lyster. I skimmed through a few of the articles. Four years ago, Harry Lyster, owner of a London-based investment firm, had been under investigation for fraud. Lyster had maintained his innocence right up until the moment he disappeared.

The name Lillian Helena Stratham wasn't listed in the headlines of the articles. It was buried in the text, usually only a line or two, and she was almost always referred to as "secretary Lillian Helena Stratham," who had been questioned. Some of the articles hinted that Lillian knew where her boss had gone. None of the articles had any pictures of Lillian, but there were plenty of Harry Lyster.

Louise had been motoring around the pub, balancing a tray of empty pint glasses, but as she passed my table, her steps checked. She leaned down to peer at the photo at the top of the news story, which showed Lyster, a heavyset man with brown hair in a suit and sunglasses, stepping into a limousine.

"Oh, I remember him," Louise said. "The Fugitive Financier, they called him. Ran some sort of scam then disappeared with millions."

I clicked over to another article with a picture of him seated at a white linen-covered table. It had been taken through a window, which caused a haze to blur his features. "Amy Brown was his secretary."

"The woman who was killed knew the Fugitive Financier?"

"Yes. She worked for him. Her name was Lillian Stratham. She was interviewed by the police and had her name in the news. That's probably why her name sounded familiar to you. I bet it was impossible to get a job after the scandal. Her name is in most of the stories, especially the ones after he disappeared with either outright accusations or hints that she was in on the scam. I bet she changed her name and moved to Manchester to get a fresh start."

"And then she ends up dead here in Nether Woodsmoor," Louise said slowly.

"That can't be a coincidence. I mean, not with the way she died—so violently."

"Blimey." Louise let out a long breath, then glanced around the pub. "Then that could mean…"

"That she recognized someone here."

We both looked back at the photo. Louise set down the tray and leaned closer. "Isn't there a better picture of him? That one is so grainy."

"Not without sunglasses or a hat. Seems he was quite fond of hats, always had his face shaded."

Louise said, "Does remind me of someone."

"I know, but I can't quite place the person," I agreed. I studied the photo, trying to figure out which individual features looked familiar. "It's the brow bone, I think."

"Hmm, yes. So prominent," Louise murmured, then her eyes widened, and she looked toward me.

We both spoke at the same time. "Felix Carrick."

CONSTABLE ALBERTSON RAN his hand slowly over his mouth as he studied the notes he'd made as I recapped what I discovered in the pub. "So you think the woman who was killed—Amy Brown—was really this Lillian Helena Stratham? And that she knew Felix Carrick, who is actually a fugitive, Harry Lyster?"

"Yes," I said. "I know it sounds improbable, but well…" I waved to my notebook and my laptop. "It's what I found."

I had come straight to the church hall from the pub. Quimby and Olney were out, but Constable Albertson had seen me from across the room as I tried to convince the officer manning the table near the door that I needed to get a message to Quimby.

"And your theories are based on…social media?" Constable Albertson looked up at me, a doubtful expression on his craggy face. He pronounced the words *social media* as if they were a dangerous, unknown quantity.

"Yes. I know it sounds a bit crazy, but she was very into it. You can find out a lot about people online, if you look at their profiles and what they post. And then there's the public notice in the *Gazette*. That's an official record, isn't it?"

"Yes, but we don't know for sure that this woman—this Amy Brown—was indeed Lillian at one time." I drew in a breath, but he held up a hand. "But seeing as you've brought all this to our attention, we'd better find out. Mind if I make copies of your notes?"

"Not at all." I handed him the notebook.

"While I do that, better forward those articles to my email." He wrote it down for me. "I'll see that he gets them."

"Excellent," I said, feeling relieved. Surely this would turn the investigation away from Alex. By the time I'd forwarded the links with the news stories, as well as the public record name change notice, Constable Albertson had returned my notebook to me. I felt as if a weight had been lifted off my shoulders.

"I looked up Felix's IMDB profile before I came down here," I added.

"His what?"

"His profile in the Internet Movie Database. It's a website with cast and crew lists. The names are searchable. There's nothing in Felix's profile older than three years. When I first met him, he said he'd recently gotten involved in the business."

Constable Albertson made a note as he muttered, "Everything is online nowadays." Then he escorted me to the door, but paused before pushing it open. "Did you run across any mention of Rafe Farraday in all your Internet searches?"

"No. That's what I thought I would find. Maybe she took his online class at some point, but she never mentioned it in any of her posts or updates."

The constable shook his head. "No, we requested the enrollment records. Amy Brown never took an online class with him."

"Perhaps she was enrolled as Lillian?"

Constable Albertson dipped his head, acknowledging the possibility. "The DCI will follow up on that, I'm sure. I'll speak to him about it before I head out on vandalism patrol."

"Thank you. Has there been more vandalism since the fire?" I asked, thinking that I hadn't heard anything about it, if there had been.

"No, not so much as a squiggle of graffiti."

"Well, that's good."

He pushed open the door and said that Quimby would probably want to speak to me later. I went out into the cool of the early evening, lost in thought. Perhaps Lillian had been bookish and studied classic English novels, but in my heart of hearts I didn't think so. Wouldn't some reference to books or reading have cropped up somewhere in Amy Brown's online discussions and dialogues? Would it be possible to regulate so closely what you said that you completely eliminated references to certain interests?

And why would she need to? If Amy Brown loved literature, that interest had nothing to do with a fugitive financier. Nothing about Jane Austen or books or reading would link her to Harry Lyster. No, the things she'd have to be careful of revealing were personal details about her prior work at an investment company and anything that would indicate she'd lived in London or known Harry Lyster, all topics that she steered clear of.

The shadows were lengthening as I crossed the green, but it was only late afternoon. There were still plenty of hours of sunlight left. I had spent quite a while in the church hall, first waiting to speak to Constable Albertson and then explaining what I'd found.

I took the short cut that ran through the bike trail parking lot.

I emerged onto the path that lined the back of the cottages, still lost in thought.

I'd wondered earlier if Felix had killed Lillian because she rebuffed his advances, but being exposed as a criminal who had bilked millions of dollars from innocent investors...well, that put things in a different light. But, again, the strange detail that wouldn't fit together was Rafe...or more specifically, Rafe's cottage. If Lillian recognized Felix Carrick as Harry Lyster and he killed her, why would he leave the body in Rafe's cottage?

Rafe himself was like a jigsaw puzzle piece that had been put away in the wrong box. He just didn't seem to fit. Apparently, he hadn't known the dead woman. I supposed that as the police searched Lillian's history, they might find a connection. Rafe and Lillian did live on different continents, but there was always the Internet. Perhaps they had connected through a dating site, but in her "Amy" persona Lillian had never mentioned using a dating site. And I was sure Rafe had other interests besides English literature. Maybe they'd connected through some other interest or hobby.

I trooped along the path, passing the gates to the back gardens. Rafe had denied knowing Amy Brown when he saw the sketch, and I'd really believed him later when he said he hadn't killed the woman. I sighed as I stepped through my gate. What did I really know about Rafe? He was a literature professor. He was attractive, glib, and charming. He liked first editions. He had questionable taste in women. And he intended to leverage the Jane Austen letters—no, he intended to leverage his first-hand knowledge of the now destroyed letters to promote himself.

I stopped short of the back door, suddenly remembering why that flash of blue and white in Rafe's messenger bag had looked familiar. It was the first edition of *The Great Gatsby*, the one that I'd watched Rafe put away in the bookshelves the day before the fire. Incredibly lucky that he'd taken it with him to the library the next day shortly before the fire destroyed the front room of his cottage, the room that had also contained the Jane Austen letters. I stood motionless, ideas darting through my mind.

Oh, yes, he was one lucky man. Maybe too lucky? He'd not only found undiscovered letters from one of literature's most famous and most beloved authors, he'd also become the sole expert on those letters once the fire destroyed them. How *incredibly* lucky that he had notes and had studied them so extensively.

I surged forward up the steps to the back door, but jerked to a stop when I spotted a pot of bright red tulips. *Where had those come from?* And the white bench with two pairs of rain boots under it?

I hastily backed down the path. This wasn't my cottage. It was the one next door. I should have noticed that latch on the gate. It moved so smoothly, not like mine that stuck and didn't want to give, but I'd been so lost in thought that I hadn't even noticed that I'd gone up the wrong path. I quickly relatched the gate and moved a few yards down the path to my gate, which looked exactly like the other gate. All the gates looked alike, and there was no variance in the low stone wall that ran the length of the path. Surprising, really, that I hadn't made the mistake before.

I was in the process of closing the gate, but paused. Someone *had* made that mistake—the murderer.

CHAPTER 16

I ATTACKED THE GATE LATCH, forcing it closed, then flew up the path to my door, but remembered at the last moment that I'd left through the front door this morning. The back would be bolted closed. I'd have to go in the front. It didn't matter, I was on my way to the front of the cottage anyway. I ducked around the side of the house through the narrow opening between the house and the yews that divided the cottage gardens then emerged into the front garden. Instead of going to my door, I went to the front of Rafe's burnt out cottage. Boards covered the front window and door, but that didn't matter. I didn't want to go inside. The ground in the front garden was still muddy from the water that the firefighters had pumped onto the fire. I carefully picked my way to the window at the front of the house, the window that had been full of flames when Alex and I arrived.

Below it, only a stump remained of what had been a large bush, which had reached all the way up to the lowest panes of the window. I looked from the window back to my cottage, remembering the sound of breaking glass I'd heard. "And no vandalism since the fire," I murmured to myself, thinking of what Constable Albertson had said. "Very clever, Rafe. Very clever."

"Did I hear my name?"

I whirled around. Rafe stood in my path. I put my hand on my heart. "Oh, Rafe. You surprised me."

"Sorry about that. What are you doing?"

"Oh, I ah—just looking around. I'm curious. It's a fault of mine."

"Want a look inside?" Rafe asked, tossing back the flap of the messenger bag and digging around inside the bag. "I still have the keys to the back door. There are some things I want to get from the kitchen. The fire didn't make it that far, so there should be a few things that are recoverable."

"Thanks, but no. Are you sure you should go in there?" I edged around him and down the path to the gate.

"I've already been inside once. Worst part is the soot, but I came prepared this time." He pulled out a pair of shoe covers and balanced on one foot as he worked the thin paper bootie over his shoe. "Surprising what they have down at the grocery, really."

"Yes," I said, then murmured to myself, "Timers and everything."

"What's that?" Rafe reached into his bag again for the other shoe cover, which shoved the edge of the bag down, revealing the book with blue letters on a white background. I tried to look away quickly and nonchalantly, but I must not have been fast enough because Rafe glanced quickly from me to the bag then hurriedly flung the flap into place.

I backed through the gate. "Sorry to run, but I have an appointment." I debated for a millisecond about whether I should try and walk casually away, but then I heard him swear, and the gate creak behind me as he followed me out.

I sprinted through my gate, digging in my pocket for my keys. "Kate! Don't go."

I shoved the key in the lock and turned it with more force

than I'd ever used. After a second's hesitation, the lock turned, and I slipped inside the door and shoved it closed in the same motion, but a solid, bootie-covered foot blocked the door from closing all the way.

"Kate, please. I can see you've worked it out. Please, let me talk to you for a moment." He didn't look so charming and care-free now. He was breathing hard, and he had a desperate look that I'd never seen on his face. He braced his palm on the door and pushed. "I'll give you a cut. Ten percent to keep this between us. Just let me explain it to you."

I shifted, putting one foot against the base of the door and leaning into it with my hip and shoulder.

"You don't have to explain anything to me. I know what happened. You faked the Jane Austen letters and then destroyed them in a fire so you'd be the only acknowledged 'expert' on them." His pressure lessened on the door, so I went on. "You orchestrated the vandalism to your window by breaking the lowest pane, the one that the bush covered, before you left—that was the breaking glass I heard, but you were all prepared with an excuse in case anyone heard. You had your story about the bottle falling out of the recycling bin ready to go. Then all you had to do was position the lamp on the throw along with the rock that would confirm the vandalism story and set the lamp on a timer."

"Kate," he said, his tone half pleading, half threatening.

"You created your alibi by working in the library and then going to the pub. No one could accuse you of arson. Except you made one mistake. You couldn't bear to let your first edition of *The Great Gatsby* burn. You had to save it. Well, that and the fact that you're so attractive that the clerk at the grocery store remembered you wanted to purchase a timer for switching lights on and off. And that's what I told the police." I figured since I'd thrown all my thoughts out there a little insurance would be a good idea.

"You didn't." He looked truly horrified. "No. No. No. That will ruin everything. I can't have that."

"I did. I was at the church hall right before I came here. I told Constable Albertson everything I knew."

Rafe seemed to have shrunk. He didn't seem so threatening, but his eyes were wild as his gaze darted around. "What am I going to do? I'll be ruined—"

I didn't wait to hear the rest of his sentence. He'd moved his foot back a fraction of an inch. I put all my weight into shoving the door. It thudded into place, and I shot the bolt home with trembling fingers.

I leaned against the door for a moment, breathing hard. The door was thick, and I couldn't hear Rafe so I crept over to the front window and peered around the edge. He stood on the path, looking around uncertainly. With his dazed expression and one bootie covering a single shoe, he looked like a drunk who'd awoken and didn't know where he was. He threw one look at my cottage then lurched down the lane toward the village.

I scurried to the back door to check the bolt in case he decided to try that door. It was locked. I slowly unhooked my tote bag from my shoulder and dropped it on the kitchen table. I found my phone and then returned to the front window. If I leaned all the way to the far side of the window, I could barely make out Rafe's figure as he paused at the end of the lane. He swayed a moment, then listed to the right and went down the short street into the village.

I let out a breath and began to run through possible ways I could explain what I'd figured out to the police. What would be the shortest, least confusing way to do it? I looked at my phone, and realized I had a text message from Alex, which had come in within the last few minutes. I hadn't heard it because my phone had been on vibrate and buried in my tote bag again.

I ignored the text, going instead to my laptop where I looked up a number for the church hall. After being transferred a few times, I reached the incident room and asked to speak to Constable Albertson.

"He's not available. Can I take a message?"

"What about DCI Quimby? Or Detective Sergeant Olney?"

There was a pause, then the man said, "I'm sorry. Neither one of them can speak to you at the moment. Your name?"

I gave my name and phone number to the man, but the thought of trying to explain that the fire was arson, and how I'd figured it out made me shake my head. *Yes, officer it was a first edition of* The Great Gatsby *that tipped me off.*

Yeah. That would take some time to explain, and to do it on the phone...not such a good idea.

I needed to go to the church hall and speak to someone in person, but I didn't want to make the walk down to the church hall on my own, since my last sighting of Rafe had been of him walking into the village.

The man assured me someone would get back to me, so I hung up, then checked the text from Alex. *Can you do me a favor and let Slink out? Caught a ride into work today because I had to drive one of the vans and now I can't get away.*

I shifted to the other side of the window and looked toward the dead end of the lane. Alex's MG was parked in front of his cottage. He probably had to move equipment from one site to another, which wouldn't be possible in his tiny car.

I hesitated a second, then texted back, an idea forming. *Sure, but I don't have a key.*

Even if the locks on the cottages could be opened without a key, I didn't want to give that a try. I'd probably be the one person in all of Nether Woodsmoor who wouldn't be able to jimmy the locks.

Great! Thxs. Key is under the third flagstone from the back door.

I quickly texted back. *Okay. I'll do it. Mind if I borrow your car afterward to run into the village?*

Within seconds, a new message from Alex downloaded. *No problem. Keys are on the table by the stairs.*

Excellent. I could drive down to the church hall locked securely in Alex's car. I'd have to deal with the seat that slid around, but I'd rather do that than run the risk of meeting Rafe face-to-face on foot or wait around for the police to return my call. It might be hours before I heard from them.

Thxs. Let's meet later. Lots to tell you.

I hurried upstairs and did a quick survey of the back garden and as much of the path and other back cottage gardens as I could see. I didn't see anyone except a woman a few cottages down from me laying out placemats on a table in her back garden. Good, if anything went wrong, I could yell for help, and she'd hear me.

I stomped down the stairs, grabbed my tote bag, and went out through my back garden. I jogged along the path to Alex's cottage. The woman setting the table looked up as I passed by. "Lovely evening," I called, and she agreed.

The gate to Alex's cottage opened smoothly, and I had no trouble prying up the flagstone to find the key. It looked like my back garden, except there were fewer flowerbeds, maybe because Alex had a dog or maybe because the tall oaks that bordered the side of the cottage cast too much shade. A well-chewed tennis ball lay in the middle of a patch of grass, and a round barbeque grill sat between two plastic chairs on a brick patio near the house.

With a last quick glance over my shoulder to confirm that the back garden was still empty, I unlocked the back door and stepped inside, then pushed the door firmly closed behind me. I paused a moment, catching my breath. It hadn't been a long distance, but in my state of hyper-awareness, my heart was skittering and my breathing was choppy.

I'd expected Slink to come trotting out to meet me, her nails clicking on the hardwood floor, but the house was quiet. "Slink. Here, Slink." Like my cottage, the back door opened directly into the kitchen, but Ivy Cottage was designed differently from my cottage. It felt a bit larger. The kitchen had more cabinets and was more spacious. Dishes were soaking in the sink, and stacks of papers ranged over the round kitchen table. Two mugs, one blue and one covered in daisies, hung on hooks behind the coffee maker.

I moved into the hallway, which was cluttered with a full laundry basket, a snowboard propped in a corner, and a collapsed umbrella. The rest of the layout of this cottage was also different than mine. The hallway in my cottage ran directly from the kitchen to the front room with only the stairs on one side, but in this cottage two doors opened off the wall opposite the stairs. The first was a bathroom, the door partially open so that I could see a tiny shower and sink.

The quiet house worried me. "Slink," I called again, louder as I moved by the bath.

No jingle of tags or padding of paws on the hardwood. I stopped abruptly as what I'd seen in the bathroom registered. I backtracked a step and pushed the door open wider. A pink and white bathrobe hung from a hook by the shower, and, as I looked closer, I saw a round brush, a blow dryer, and hair clips scattered along the storage shelf next to the sink as well as a pink toothbrush in the holder.

What was going on? That was a decidedly feminine robe and the hair accessories...the items added up to a woman in Alex's house, but that couldn't be right. Alex was single...wasn't he? Why would he be flirting with me and asking me out to dinner and *kissing* me, if there was a pink bathrobe hanging in his bathroom? *But there had been that hair scrunchy in his car, too.* And he had almost told me something after we kissed, but he'd caught himself and said that it wasn't the right time.

I crossed my arms. So he was either married or had someone who was comfortable enough in Ivy Cottage to leave her bathrobe and hair styling stuff strewn around the bathroom. But how could that be? Nether Woodsmoor was tiny. If he was married or living with someone, people would know. *Someone* would have said something. And how could I not have seen her coming and going from the cottage? We lived on the same street.

I spun away from the bathroom. Alex's love life didn't matter right now. I needed to take care of Slink and get to the church hall. "Slink," I called again as I searched a narrow table that stood near the stairs covered with junk mail, a leash, and framed snapshots. Sticky notes dotted the table and spotted the wall. I found the key ring under a tilting stack of envelopes and catalogues.

I shook the keys and called for Slink again over the jingling sound, but the house was silent. Seriously worried, I moved to the middle of the hall, debating for a second if I should explore the house or just get out of there. Alex had told me that between her bursts of energy, Slink spent a lot of time sleeping, but what dog didn't come running when you jangled a set of car keys and called its name?

Getting out seemed to be the best thing to do. Something was wrong—and it had nothing to do with the pink bathrobe and other signs of female habitation. I strode quickly for the front door, the car keys gripped in my hand, but a man stepped out of the front room and blocked my path.

"Mr. Lyons, what are you—"

I jerked to a stop as I saw the gun he held trained on me. My heartbeat kicked up again as I backed up a step. I would have gone farther, but he raised his eyebrows and held up his free hand, palm out like a cop stopping traffic.

I didn't move an inch more, but my mind—along with my heart rate—raced along. *Hector Lyons in Alex's house? Pointing a gun at me? Pink bathrobes and no Slink? What was going on?*

"No use continuing my little charade, is there?" He'd changed out of the biking gear and now had on a black t-shirt, dark pants, and sturdy rubber-soled black shoes. He removed his glasses, slipped them into his pants pocket and brushed his long bangs to the side, revealing a protruding brow. "You know who I am, don't you?"

Without the glasses and the hair in the way, I could see it now. He'd lost weight—lots of weight. Probably fifty pounds or more. His face was slimmer, his cheeks more hollow than in the photos I'd seen of Harry Lyster. It was amazing how much weight loss changed a person's appearance. His hair was different, too. Lighter, a golden color instead of dark brown, and threaded with gray. He had altered something else, too. Something that was different from even the last time I'd seen him at the pub. In my on-edge, hyper-aware state it only took me a second to figure it out: he'd shaved off his mustache and beard.

I figured it wouldn't do any good to play dumb, even if I'd only figured it out seconds earlier. He thought that I knew who he was. He'd been in the pub when I was talking to Louise and either overheard us talking or seen what I was searching for on my computer. "Yes, you're Harry Lyster." My voice came out quivery. I sucked in a deep breath, trying to counter my pounding heart and shallow breaths.

"You should be proud of yourself. In three years, you're only the second person to figure it out."

He's talking about Amy—no Lillian. Lillian was her real name, I thought, a memory of the fire licking out of Rafe's cottage window and up to the roof popping into my mind. My pulse went into the stratospheric range. Harry was the one who'd killed Lillian and put her in Rafe's cottage, not Felix. How stupid I'd been to jump to the conclusion that the murderer was Felix based on one physical characteristic. Look at how much Harry had managed to change his appearance, camouflaging the things that were hard to change, like his brow bone, but using other things like weight loss, a beard, a mustache, glasses, and a new hairstyle—even a new hair color—to look like a different person.

"And you didn't know me before. Lilly worked for me. She

had an advantage over you, so it's quite impressive that you managed to figure it out on your own."

"Alex knows that I'm here," I said quickly. If this man had killed once to keep his secret, I didn't think he'd have any qualms about doing it again.

He gave me a pitying look. "No, that was me."

"I have texts on my phone from Alex. I'll show you." I slowly lifted my hand toward my tote bag.

Harry made a little tsking sound. "So gullible," he said on a sigh. "It's incredible how easy it is to fool people these days. Everyone trusts their technology, their phones and computers, but it wasn't a text from Alex. It was from me. I cloned his phone."

"You cloned his phone?" I said slowly. Unlike Rafe, who had looked on the verge of doing something crazy, Harry looked completely calm and in control of himself, but maybe he wasn't all there, mentally. "How would you do that?" I asked, half expecting the answer to be something woo-woo about positive energy flow or magnetic fields.

"Cell phone signal booster. They're quite common now, and so simple to hack. Once I had his phone details, I could listen in on his calls, monitor his texts, even send texts that looked like they came from his phone."

I revised my assessment. He was perfectly lucid. "I see. Sounds like you know what you're talking about."

I scanned the cottage, trying to think what I could do. The front door was directly behind him, so I wasn't going that way. If I sprinted for the back door, he'd have a clear shot at me since the hall ran straight and true down the short distance to the kitchen. Going upstairs wouldn't help. I'd only be trapped up there. The bathroom door was slightly behind me and to my right. Could I make it in there, slam the door, and climb out the window? I remembered light coming in from the shower, but how big had the window been? I'd been so focused on the pink robe that I hadn't noticed the size of the window. And would the door hold? Could he fire the gun through the lock to get inside? Sleek and squared off, the gun wasn't much bigger than his hand, but it looked sturdy and lethal.

"Quite handy," he continued. "I've cloned most of my neighbor's cell phones and a few phones that belong to strategic citizens. So important to know what Constable Albertson is relaying to his superiors. Got to love technology."

I felt a sinking sensation in my gut. No one knew I was here, and I had no hope of bluffing my way out. If Harry did have access to Constable Albertson's phone, he'd know exactly what I'd told the police.

"Oh, don't look like that. I'm not going to hurt you. You're my ticket out of here."

CHAPTER 17

"*R*EALLY?" I ASKED, AND I'M afraid that despite my fear the word came out a tad sarcastic. While I believed what he said about technology, I wasn't about to trust anything else he said.

"Oh, yes. It's true. I need you." He pulled his phone from his pocket and checked it. "It's playing out just as I thought it would."

He turned the screen toward me, and I saw it was divided into four sections. Black and white images moved on two of the sections. In one, a four-door sedan moved slowly up a long, tree-shaded drive. In another, a flicker of movement showed two men in police uniforms drop over a stone wall and crouch down. Staying in their hunched position, the men moved out of camera range.

"My house," he explained. He turned the screen back toward him and shook his head. "They've decided to go in quietly, as I thought they would. No sirens. They don't want to spook me, but I'm already several steps ahead of them." He pointed the phone to a brown leather holdall bag resting beside the front door.

"Once I knew they were coming, I cleared out. I always have a bag ready, but I couldn't go in my car, so I came down here to pick up Alex's car because the police are setting up roadblocks on the two roads out of Nether Woodsmoor. I knew from Alex's texts that he didn't have his car with him today—I monitor things like that. So important to know what your options are at all times, don't you think? An exit strategy is everything, you know. Anyway, I knew I'd be able to find his keys, or worst case, hot wire his car myself. It's an older car so it shouldn't be hard to do, but then I had the inspiration of bringing you in."

He slipped his phone into his pocket, then reached for Alex's light gray windbreaker and worked one arm into the sleeve, never letting the gun waver from me. He switched the gun to the other hand, and pulled the jacket on his other arm. "Looks like rain, don't you think?" He settled the jacket on his shoulders, then picked up a worn denim baseball cap that hung on another peg, working it onto his head.

"With you in the driver's seat, we'll zip through the road block —" he paused, put his hand on his chest. "Flattering really, that they've gone to the trouble, but in the end it won't matter. It's known around the village that you sometimes drive Alex's car. You even mentioned it to the police at the church hall the other day. I was there and heard you along with several other officers. In Alex's jacket and hat, I'll pass a cursory look, I think." He shot a quick look at himself in the mirror hanging above the narrow table in the hall and gave the brim of the hat a quick adjustment.

He took a step back and grabbed the handle of the front door. "Shall we?"

I didn't move.

He raised his eyebrows. "You don't like my plan?"

"No, considering that I can't possibly be useful to you," I swallowed, but managed to continue, "after you're out of Nether Woodsmoor. I'm sure that if you have a bag packed and monitor your property, then you most likely have an escape plan that will take you out of the U.K., and I doubt that plan involves a traveling companion. No, I'd be something you had to discard, excess baggage as it were," I said, matching his light tone.

"Kate." He dipped his chin and gave me a hurt look. "I'm not going to harm you. I don't need anything else on my plate. You drive me to Upper Benning, drop me at the train station, and you're done."

"You'll let me drive away? Just like that?"

"Yes, exactly like that. Once I'm on the train, I'm home free. I have a new identity that can't be tracked. I only need you to get out of Nether Woodsmoor. I'm not some sort of monster."

I licked my lips. "Then where's Slink?"

"Slink? Oh, the dog." He motioned to the front room. "On her cushion, sleeping off a rather large lunch."

I took a step forward, then jerked to a stop, remembering the gun.

He motioned me into the room with the gun. "Go ahead, take a look."

I hesitated for a second, then went across the room to the circular dog cushion placed next to the couch. Slink was indeed out, her massive chest rising and falling with each breath, her long limbs loose and relaxed as they draped over the edge of the squashy cushion.

"I had a very nice steak in my refrigerator. She quite enjoyed it. I couldn't have her snapping and growling at me when I came in the back door unexpectedly. Handy to know where Alex hid his spare key as well. I didn't even have to force the lock."

I ran my hand over her soft short fur, and Slink stirred, opened her eyes and tilted her head toward me. I rubbed her head and one silky ear. She dropped her head back to the cushion with a sigh. I wasn't sure I believed that only a full stomach had made her so lethargic. I bet that he put something else—some sort of sedative or medicine in with the food—but she did seem to be okay, just sleepy. I could feel her steady heartbeat as I petted her, and her breathing was even.

"She warmed up to me quickly, once she smelled the steak." Harry said. "Now, that you can see that I'm not some sort of brute, can we leave?"

I ran my hand along Slink's side once more, trying to scan the room for anything that I could use to get myself out of this awful situation, but the fireplace tools were too far away to lunge for, and the only other things within reach was a remote control and a glossy gossip magazine that had been left on the couch cushions.

He tapped his watch. "Time is ticking." His affable tone had faded. Now his words were sharp. "You can be useful to me, or you can be an obstacle. Much better to be useful."

I stood and walked toward the front door, the keys gripped in my hand.

He glanced down at my hand as he picked up his bag. "Don't think you can attack me and get away. I've had nothing but time on my hands for three years and done extensive self-defense training. You strike me—or *try* to strike me—and you'll regret it."

"Wouldn't dream of it." Before he'd slipped on Alex's jacket, the tight t-shirt he wore revealed a toned and in-shape physique. He was a careful and thorough man. I didn't doubt that he had prepared himself in every way he could to avoid capture.

I didn't think for a minute that he would let me go, but I had zero self-defense skills. I wasn't about to take him on directly. No, my best bet was to get away from him outside the cottage. He'd be more reluctant to fire the gun outside in full view of several houses. "I'll get you to that train station so you can get on your way."

"Brilliant. Lead on." He picked up the holdall and tucked the gun into my ribcage as I opened the door. If there had been anyone on the street who knew me, they would have immediately noticed us and probably thought it was odd how we moved down the path in lockstep, our bodies only inches from each other, his body bumping up against me. I tried to create some distance between us, but he dug the gun deeper into my side. "Don't move away. Stay close." His voice was tense now. We moved around the gate in a weird shuffle. "Open the trunk," he commanded.

I popped it open, and he cursed under his breath. The trunk was stuffed with a mishmash of items. Tools, a soccer ball, a wadded blanket, sheaves of paper, and a raincoat were on the top layer and filled the trunk to the brim. There was no way he was fitting his holdall in there, and there was no backseat to toss it in either.

"Never mind. Close it."

I pushed down the lid, and he directed me around to the passenger side. I could feel his choppy breath pushing against my hair as he glanced up and down the empty street. "Open the door, and get in."

I followed instructions, relieved to get away from the gun and his clinging body. A flash of light hit the rearview mirror, and I caught a glimpse of a car turning onto the street. I thought he'd slam the door and go around to the other side. This could be my chance to run. I'd wait until he was on the far side of the car. He wouldn't shoot—not with another car on the road—that would draw attention to him, and attention was the last thing he wanted.

But he didn't go around, he stayed beside me. Now the gun was in the pocket of his jacket, but I could tell from the way the fabric strained that it was still aimed at me. "Go on. Crawl over to the driver's side."

It wasn't easy to do in the tiny space, but I scrambled over the stick shift and settled into the driver's seat, my gaze immediately went to the mirrors. I could still get out—go out the driver's door and keep the MG between us until the car came to this end of the street. I hesitated, checking the mirrors for the car that had been on the road, but it had parked in front of the first cottage on the street, and I could just make out a figure as it moved up the steps to the front door and disappeared inside. The street was now completely empty.

I dropped my hand from the door handle as Harry slid inside. "Very good. Now, start the car and make a U-turn, nice and smooth."

I adjusted the seat forward so that I could reach the pedals, still scanning the mirrors, hoping someone would emerge from one of the cottages. Didn't someone need to take their dog for a walk or run to the store?

"What are you waiting on?" He was obviously glad to be inside the car. He didn't sound quite as edgy as he had on the street. "Let's go."

"Right."

I put the car in gear, and with only a few shudders as I worked the gas and clutch, I made it through the U-turn and cruised to the end of the lane.

"Signal," he commanded as I stopped.

I dutifully flicked on the blinker and made the turn, driving down the short street and then signaling again as I worked my way into the village. "Go to the high street, then follow the main road over the bridge and out of town after the roundabout. Don't speed. Everything nice and legal." He settled back, relaxing as we cruised smoothly through the streets, hitting the few traffic lights green. I concentrated on staying on the correct side of the road, my hands clenched on the wheel.

We sailed over the bridge and into the open countryside, the road rising and falling gently with the undulating curves of the land. We hit a gentle climb, and I felt the car seat shift, giving a little, and I remembered how it had slid backward the other time I'd driven it. I'd completely forgotten about it. Alex hadn't had time to get it fixed. The hill was a small one. We crested it and were on the way back down before the seat slipped out of its position. The rise in elevation had given us a glimpse down the road, and I could see a curving trail of red brake lights.

"That will be the roadblock," he said.

I knew what I had to do. The next rise was higher.

I didn't know the roads well enough around Nether Woodsmoor to know if I'd have another opportunity. It had to be now. I'd hesitated earlier in the street in front of the cottage and missed a chance. This might be the only other break I got.

"Relax your hands on the wheel. When we get to the front of the line, you do the talking. I'll keep my head down, but don't forget I'll have the gun—"

I stamped on the accelerator as we reached the base of the hill.

My seat flew backward. With fumbling fingers, I unlocked the seat belt and shoved the door open. The sound of the tires and the wind filled the car. Harry shouted something. I had a quick impression of the road as it flew by, dark and glittery black, until it met a thick layer of grass.

Harry's hand clamped down on my shoulder. I twisted to the side and saw the car door falling back toward me. I put out a hand and writhed away from Harry's grasping fingers, shifting toward the door. I heaved myself toward it, more to block it from closing on me than to throw myself out, but the next thing I felt was a crushing impact along my shoulder and arm. Then my breath was gone and the sky and ground were spinning around as I thumped and bumped along like a ragdoll.

When I stopped rolling, I fought to get air back into my lungs. Gasping and gulping, I managed to push myself up and get my face out of the grass. The sound of a horn filled the air, and I looked up in time to see the little red MG, which had crossed the line into oncoming traffic, jerk back into its lane. Harry must have overcorrected because the car careened back across the centerline and bumped off the road, hitting the grass and taking the downward slope, picking up speed and angling away from me toward a stone wall that cut across the field.

He turned the car again, and it spun. But he was too close to the wall, and the tires couldn't get any traction on the slick grass. The back end of the car slammed into the stone wall in a thud of crunching metal that made me cringe.

"Oh, Alex. You're going to need to do more than fix the seat in the car," I murmured as I slowly rolled into a sitting position. But then I remembered how many questions I had for Alex, and my sympathies dropped away.

Everything ached, but I was able to move my hands and flex my feet back and forth so it didn't seem that I'd done any severe damage to myself. I shifted slowly to my feet, keeping an eye on the MG, but no one emerged from it.

A few cars had pulled to the side of the road, and a figure was moving down the hill toward me. "I'm okay," I called then spotted a police car rolling to a stop at the top of the rise where the MG had left the road.

I trudged up the hill, every step sending painful vibrations through me. I waved, catching the attention of the policeman who'd stepped from his car. I pointed to the red car. "He's the one you're looking for. That's Harry—I mean, Hector Lyons. And he's got a gun."

I'd never seen a reaction quite like I got from the police officer. He went back to his car and, within a few minutes, the red car was surrounded.

CHAPTER 18

"OUT COLD," CONSTABLE ALBERTSON SAID to me a few hours later as he handed me a cup of tea. "Looks like the impact with the stone wall threw him forward, causing him to hit his head on the dash. He's in hospital now, but as soon as he's awake, we'll have a go at him."

We were back in the church hall, which was bustling with activity, even though it was after midnight. It had taken a long time to sort out the scene after Harry ran into the stone wall. "So, he'll be okay?"

"Oh, yes. The doctors say he'll be out in a few days. Of course, that will mean a transfer to jail until he can answer for the death here. And then there's the fraud case."

"Oh, what about Slink?" I'd told the first police officer I'd talked to about Slink. He'd assured me someone would check on her.

"I got in touch with Alex Norcutt. He's taken her to the vet and says no harm was done. Should be back to her normal self tomorrow."

"That's good." A flutter of commotion drew my attention to the side door where Quimby had arrived. He talked with a few people, but then came directly over to me. "Well. In the thick of it again. Are you feeling all right?"

"Aside from some aches and pains, I'm okay. Apparently, I'll really feel it tomorrow." At least that's what the first responders had told me. They had wanted to transfer me to the hospital along with Harry, but I'd refused to go for two reasons. I didn't want to be anywhere near Harry, and I had no idea how I'd pay for a hospital visit. The U.K. might have socialized medicine, but I doubted it extended to unemployed Americans who happened to be in the country. My funds were already tight enough. I promised to get medical attention at the first sign of headache, double vision, or any other unusual condition.

Quimby motioned for me to follow him to the office down the hall. Once we were seated there, he asked me to take him through what had happened.

"I suppose I should start with Rafe."

"Rafe?"

"Yes."

Quimby consulted a screen on his phone. "But my understanding was that you came here earlier today to report the connections you'd made about Amy Brown being Lillian Stratham."

"Yes. That was what I figured out in the pub. I came straight here and told Constable Albertson everything. I was on my way home when I worked out the rest. It was *The Great Gatsby*. If I hadn't seen it in Rafe's messenger bag, I probably never would have figured it out."

I told him how once I'd realized the book was the first edition everything else fell into place. "The timer Rafe had wanted to purchase, the sound of breaking glass on the day of the fire, how the vandalism stopped after the fire. He'd carefully set everything up so that the fire would destroy the 'letters,' leaving him as the sole authority on them. And I bet he staged the vandalism around the village so that the fire would be thought of as another incident. He met with a publicist this afternoon. They were discussing a huge media campaign, both here and in the United States. He intended to use the fake letters to launch him to an even higher level of fame."

"So you confronted him with this information?"

"Oh no. I mean, I didn't intend to. The pieces were still coming together. I'd accidentally gone inside the wrong back garden on my way home. I was thinking about a flash of blue letters on white that I'd seen inside Rafe's messenger bag at the pub. I'd just worked out it was his first edition of *The Great Gatsby*. I was so lost in thought that I went in the wrong back gate. I realized that's what the murderer must have done."

I'd had a lot of time to wait out on the stretch of green countryside while the accident scene was cleared away. Working out what must have happened was a good mental exercise to keep me from fixating on how badly things could have turned out tonight.

"Harry must have killed Lillian, either on the path behind the cottages or at his home," I said. "I saw her walking that direction. It makes sense that she was going to see him. If she actually visited him at his house, I could see him waiting until she left, then following her and killing her on the path. Plenty of rocks to use as a weapon." I paused and blew out a breath, not liking the images the words created. "He probably intended to stash her body in what, up until the day before, had been an unoccupied cottage, my cottage. I'd only been in it one day and hardly home at all, so he might not have realized I'd moved in. Anyway, the locks are easy to force, so he probably planned to leave her body there until later, after dark. The layout and design of my cottage and Rafe's are identical. I didn't have anything in mine that would show someone had just moved in. No boxes or packing paper or even a suitcase left out."

"So you think he put the body in Rafe's cottage by mistake?"

"Yes. I made the same mistake myself. I walked up to the back door of the cottage next door before I realized it was the wrong one. The back gates and gardens are similar and neither Rafe nor I have anything outside that would identify our cottages. But before Hector—I mean Harry—could retrieve the body, Rafe's timer turned on the light, which set fire to his cottage. Since Lillian's body had been placed in his cottage, the death was discovered that night. Of course, I hadn't worked out the whole thing. I didn't realize it was Harry. I was still figuring out what Rafe had done."

"Take me through that."

"I went inside Rafe's front garden to look at his window, and he appeared behind me. It seemed like that. I never heard him coming. I was probably so absorbed in my thoughts that I didn't hear him." I explained about seeing the first edition again. "I tried not to show that I'd noticed it, but he must have seen it in my face. He offered me a cut, ten percent, to keep quiet, but I told him I'd already told the police about it. It was a bluff, but I figured it was better for me, if he thought the secret was out."

"Glad we could be of some help to you," Quimby said dryly. "Go on. What happened next?"

"I managed to get inside my cottage and lock him out. He left, wandering off with a dazed look. Do you know where he is?"

"Yes, he was taken into custody in Manchester. He was trying to get on the last flight of the day. He will answer for the arson, but let's finish your narrative before we get into that. After Mr. Farraday left, what did you do?"

"Well, I intended to come down here, but I got a text from Alex. At least, I thought it was from Alex." I recounted Harry's boasts about cloning phones.

Quimby's face got darker and more closed off the more I told him. "One moment." He left the room, but was back within five minutes. "I have my tech people on it. They say what he described is possible. It was my understanding that you thought it was Felix Carrick who was the murderer."

"Yes. It was his protruding brow bone. Stupid of me to think that Harry wouldn't have done more to conceal his identity." I recounted what had happened and ended with my tumble through the field. Quimby had a few follow-up questions, but not many. I thought he must be going easy on me because I had mud and grass sticking out of my hair and was huddled inside a borrowed jacket because the sleeve and back of my shirt had been shredded when I went flying out of the car.

"Okay, that's all for now. We'll have more questions, but those can wait. Let's get you home."

"Wait, can you tell me how you zeroed in on Harry so quickly? I mean, I'm really glad that your officers knew exactly who Harry was when I mentioned his name, and didn't mess around making sure he wasn't going to come out of the car, gun blazing."

Quimby pressed his lips together for a moment, then said, "I suppose you, of all people, deserve to see this." He tapped a few keys on the laptop in front of him as he spoke. "What you told Constable Albertson set us on the right track. Once we had the connection between Amy Brown and Lillian Stratham, we dug into her background. Like you, we considered men in the village who fit the age and physical profile we were looking for, but then this came in."

He turned it so that I could see a picture of Lillian, the beginning of a video, which filled the screen.

CHAPTER 19

I GLANCED BACK AT QUIMBY, my eyebrows raised. "What's this?"

"A video that Lillian made after her first visit to Nether Woodsmoor. We just got access to it today. Our tech people had her desktop computer, but they were focused on her email and files. Lillian recorded this video through Legacy.com, a website that helps people handle their online accounts after their death."

"Oh, I've heard about those types of sites," I said. "You can name someone to take over your email and social media accounts." When I'd read an article about them, I'd thought that having something like that would be a good idea, but I hadn't actually set up an account, putting it off as one of those things that I'd do later. But Lillian's job revolved around social media and online activities, so I wasn't surprised that she had lined up a service like that.

"Right, an online beneficiary. Lillian had named a colleague at work. Once we identified the body as Amy Brown on Wednesday and notified her office, her colleague told us about the account, but she couldn't get access until she had a death certificate. We were able to expedite the process, but it still took until today to get full access. From the internal information we received from Legacy.com, Lillian logged in to her account on Monday evening from work, made this video, and changed her account settings so that if she died, this video would be emailed to a selected list of recipients, which included her colleague as well as the Nether Woodsmoor police." Quimby tapped a key and the video began.

It looked as if she were recording it in her home, maybe an apartment. The lighting was a bit dim and, in the background, I could see bookshelves and a pale green waterproof jacket thrown over the arm of a chair.

I hadn't got a good look at her on the path behind the cottages that day when I was struggling to get the gate to latch, but now that the camera was focused on her in a close-up, I could see that besides long, light-blond hair, she had darker eyebrows that slashed straight across her forehead above brown eyes and a slightly upturned nose.

Lillian cleared her throat and squared her shoulders. "Well, if anyone is watching this that means my plan didn't go so well." She cleared her throat again. She must have been sitting in an office chair because she swiveled, and her shoulders rotated from side to side. "I suppose I should start with my name. I go by Amy Brown now, but I used to be Lillian Stratham. I changed my name. It's all legal and everything, but after what happened, it was impossible to even get a call back, much less an interview."

She stopped, looked down at the desktop. "Right. I'm making a hash of this, but hopefully no one will ever see it, so it doesn't matter. Back to Lillian. When I was Lillian, I worked for Harry Lyster. Yes, *that* Harry Lyster. The Fugitive Financier."

She shook her head and blew out a sigh. "He had us all so fooled. We had no idea he was running a scam. At least, I didn't, but the police didn't believe that. I was his secretary, so they thought I would know exactly what had gone on. I didn't." She said the last words firmly. "But that didn't matter. And it didn't matter that the police never charged me with anything.

Employers saw my name, and they moved my resume into the 'no' pile. So I changed my name and moved to Manchester. Started over, literally working my way up from the receptionist to the job I have now, managing social media." She glanced away as she murmured, "At least that was one thing I learned, media manipulation."

She refocused on the camera. "So last weekend there I was, going through my life, taking a weekend in the country for a bike race—I've taken it up—when I saw Harry." Her face changed. Her brows lowered and her lips pressed together for a moment. "He was suited up for the bike race, not three feet away from me. He looked different. So much slimmer. And his hair was different, too. I thought it was him, but I wasn't one hundred percent sure, so I watched him. I stayed near him throughout the race—but not so close that I drew his attention. Then after it was over, I followed him back to the local pub.

"He had a pint then picked up a takeaway meal. By then, I was pretty sure, but when I saw him tap the bar twice with his knuckle as he said good-bye to the person who'd brought his food, I knew it was him." Satisfaction laced her tone. "He used to do that at the end of every meeting, the little rap on the table right before he left. He'd worked hard to change his appearance, but he hadn't changed his mannerisms."

I glanced at Quimby. "Weird," I said. "He did the same thing the other day at the pub, the first time I met him."

Quimby nodded as the video continued. Lillian's face broke into a slow grin. She tilted her chin upward. "The bar was crowded, so he didn't notice me, and I made sure he didn't see me follow him home." The grin dropped from her face. "He lived in a *mansion*." Anger vibrated through her tone. "So unfair. I was wiped out, penniless, after Harry disappeared. I had to use every-thing I had to hire a solicitor, all because of what Harry did. I wasn't guilty. He was. But I was the one who had my reputation smeared and ended up with nothing. *Nothing*," she repeated, leaning toward the camera, her face filling every inch of the screen.

She fell back in her chair and ran her hands through her hair, visibly calming down. "So he owes me. I'm going back to Nether Woodsmoor tomorrow and tell him he's going to pay me a nice little bonus, something to make up for all the trouble he's caused me."

She looked away from the camera a moment, then nodded. "Yeah, that's about it. I have no doubt that he'll pay up. He's basically a coward. He always was more talk than action. This video is my insurance policy. If I'm not back home," she paused and smiled, "with a much bigger bank balance, then this video will be released. Harry will pay, one way or the other."

The video ended there, and I turned to Quimby, stunned. "So she tried to blackmail him."

Quimby closed the laptop. "I believe so. We don't have any confirmation of this video, but when she returned here, Harry may have recognized her and killed her."

"Or, she confronted him, and he didn't believe she had left a message that would expose him. She really didn't sound like she was worried about him hurting her."

Quimby said, "She remembered the façade that he presented when he worked in London, the con man. He'd managed to hide his identity for years. Perhaps he wouldn't have resorted to murder three years ago, but now...well, let's just say that three years of watching your back every moment changes a person. He had no real contacts here. It's my understanding that he isolated himself from the community, only occasionally participating in the bike races."

"And helping with the wall restoration project," I said slowly.

Quimby frowned. "What project?"

I explained about how the historical preservation society had rebuilt the wall along the path. "I was with Beatrice when she personally thanked him for his help and tried to get him involved with another project, but he wasn't interested. At the time I didn't think anything about it, but now, knowing what we know, it does seem odd." A thought flitted through my mind—something peripherally related to our conversation—but before I could grasp it, it was gone. I wasn't exactly at my sharpest. I was tired and drained now that the adrenaline was out of my system. I realized that Quimby had gone on to another topic and dragged my mind back to what he was saying.

"...need tests to confirm it, but the gun Lyster was carrying matches the type of bullets fired at you yesterday."

I blinked. "But why? Why would he shoot at me? I was completely wrong in who I thought was the murderer. I didn't even suspect him. And I only figured out about Amy being Lillian earlier today."

Quimby opened a file and flicked through some papers. "You came in yesterday afternoon to sign your statement about seeing Lillian on the path behind the cottages."

"Yes." That seemed like it had been several days ago.

Quimby switched to another paper. "Harry Lyster was here at the same time, giving his statement about seeing Rafe at the pub."

"Oh, that's right. He was at the table near the door."

"And did you mention that you had seen the woman on the path behind the cottages?"

"Yes, I think I did when I first came in."

"He must have overheard and assumed that there was a possibility you had seen him as well."

"But I didn't see him."

"But he couldn't be sure. He assumed that you were a threat to him. Slipping into and out of the woods during the filming the next day wouldn't have been hard. All he had to do was wait until you were in view and take aim. Fortunately, he wasn't a good shot."

"Lucky me," I said weakly.

Quimby stacked the papers and folded his hands on top.

"We'll be in touch once we have the final ballistic report, but I'm fairly confident of what the findings will be."

"Okay, thanks. I guess." I shook my head and sighed. "It's just a lot to take in...I'm still trying to wrap my mind around the mousy computer guy being a slick con man. I've had several hours to think about it, but it still is hard to grasp."

"The freelance computer programmer thing was completely bogus, a convenient cover for his solitary lifestyle."

"But the thing about hacking into the cell phone booster? Wouldn't he have to have some computer abilities to do that?"

"You'd be surprised what you can learn through YouTube videos. We'll probably find that he accessed some hacking forum or found step-by-step instructions posted somewhere on the Internet. It will take a while to sort out how he did it, but he didn't have any computer programming clients, *any* sort of accounts—receivable or payable—and he certainly didn't pay anything to Revenue and Customs."

"Then how did he survive? What did he live on?"

"Offshore accounts, it looks like. It will take time to dig into all his finances." Quimby stood. "You look knackered. Let me get you a ride back to your cottage."

"Thanks." I stood and followed him slowly down the hall, my mind spinning with everything we'd talked about. There was something slightly off. Something about Harry and the stone wall. Why would he do something so out of character? And there had been someone else...someone who'd acted in an unusual way. Earlier, when Quimby was talking, the comparison had flashed through my mind, but I hadn't been quick enough to latch onto it.

Quimby gestured to a chair along the wall and left me ruminating. He returned in a few minutes, a woman in uniform following him. "Ms. Sharp, PCSO Robertson will see you home."

"Rafe and Harry," I said.

"I'm sorry?"

"That's it. Rafe and Harry." I stood up. "They both behaved in unusual ways over the last few days. That's what bothered me. Rafe spent the afternoon in the library, but the librarian said he never came in or did research there. He acted uncharacteristically to create an alibi for himself so he wouldn't be accused of arson. Harry helped the historical society rebuild the stone wall. He didn't normally join in activities, and he made it clear to Beatrice that he didn't want to do anything else with the historical society."

Quimby stared at me a moment, then said. "So what was his motivation?"

"I don't know, but why would he suddenly participate?"

"Yes, it is out of character. I'll have it checked out." Quimby nodded to the woman standing by his side, and she pointed me toward the door. "This way. We'll have you home in a jiffy."

We drove back to the cottage in silence. The rest of the cottages were dark as she rolled to a stop in front of my gate. "This is the one?"

"Yes, it is. Thank you."

"Would you like me to come in, have a look around?"

"No, that's not—actually, yes, I would."

She stepped through the front door as soon as I unlocked it. I could hear her moving through the cottage. Windows glowed as she made her way upstairs. She returned to the front door. "All fine."

"Thanks. It's been quite a day. Still feeling a little off kilter from everything that has happened and trying to process that a murderer lived just down the path behind the cottages."

"No worries," she said. "I've seen it time and again. Just goes to show how hard it is to really know someone."

"Yes, it does," I said, thinking of Alex as I closed the door.

CHAPTER 20

$\mathcal{I}$ CAME DOWN THE STAIRS as carefully as a very old woman late the next morning. Every inch of me ached, but a hot shower had helped, and I planned to down some pain medicine as soon as I polished off a bowl of cereal. Coffee helped tremendously, too. I'd opened my laptop and settled into a kitchen chair, prepared to purchase my return airfare, when there was a knock on the front door. I heaved myself out of my chair and hobbled creakily to the front window. The doors didn't have peepholes, and I wasn't about to open it without knowing who it was. I expected to see a police car parked in front of the cottage, but the lane was empty. I couldn't see the front step.

"Kate? Are you home?"

It was Alex. I leaned against the wall for a moment, then trudged to the front door, but didn't open it. "Yes, I'm home, but I don't want to talk to you. You lied to me."

I thought he'd left, which should have been exactly what I wanted, but for some reason, the mental image of him walking away from my cottage didn't give me a relieved feeling. After a few seconds, he said something, and I had to strain to hear him through the thick door.

195

"...never lied to you. I promise you that."

Anger flared through me. "Didn't lie to me? Alex, I've been inside your house."

"It's not what you think, not what it looks like. Could we please not do this through a closed door?"

Reluctantly, I opened the door a few inches.

"Hey," he said, his face somber.

"Hey." I should have left the door closed. His dark eyes had shadows under them and reminded me of Slink's soulful, pleading gaze.

"I know you've been through a lot—I'm glad you're okay, by the way—you are okay, aren't you?"

"I'm getting a little preview of what it will be like to be in my nineties, I think, but I should be back to normal in a few days...or maybe weeks."

"Oh. Sorry to hear that."

"Thanks. Sorry about your car."

"Don't worry about that. It was just a car."

I looked over his shoulder, away from his sympathetic face. "You're being way too nice. You loved that car."

He lifted one shoulder. "People are more important than cars. Besides, it was insured. It'll keep Jeremy and his dad down at the garage in business for a couple of months."

"And Slink's okay?"

He whistled. I hadn't noticed the long leash gripped in his hand. Slink had been sniffing around the flowerbeds, but at his whistle, she trotted over, leaping over the steps in one fluid motion. She stopped in front of me, her head positioned exactly by my hand. I sent him an exasperated look. "Right. Bringing the dog. Clever." I ran my hand along the side of her head, caressing her ear and then down her side, which was expanding and contracting like a bellow. Alex had obviously taken her out and let her run. Slink fixed her adoring brown gaze on my face, her mouth open in a doggie grin as she panted. "You look completely recovered," I said to her. Her long tail whipped from side to side, slapping against the back of Alex's legs.

"Shouldn't you be at work?" I asked Alex.

"Today's Saturday. Scheduled day off."

"Right." I gave Slink one last rub, then stood and crossed my arms. "I'm glad Slink is okay, and I truly am sorry about your car, but the fact remains that you live with a woman. You stood right here and kissed me like...like..." I felt my cheeks heat as I remembered that kiss.

For a second, I thought I saw one corner of Alex's mouth turn up, which revived that flare of anger I'd felt before. "And you think it's funny," I said, outraged. "You are not at all the person I thought you were."

I reached to slam the door, but Alex stepped closer, his face serious. "No, wait. I kissed you the way I did because I like you, and I wanted more." He leaned closer, and I was enveloped in the scent of laundry detergent. My pulse thumped as he closed the distance. I was a mess. Intellectually, I was furious at him, but my body hadn't gotten the memo. And what was wrong with me that the smell of laundry soap made my heartbeat go crazy?

"But you're right. There's something about me that you don't know. Will you let me show you something? I think it will explain everything, and if you're still mad, well, I can accept that."

There was something in his tone that cut off my flat denial. He looked hopeful, scared, and resigned, all at the same time. "It will only take a second," he said.

I blew out a breath. "Okay."

"Great. It's at my cottage."

I nodded. "Let me get my keys." I went back to the kitchen, my internal dialogue screaming at me that I was an idiot. I wanted to whisper back. "Yes, I'm an idiot, but if I don't go I'll always wonder, *what if I'd gone?*"

I returned to the door, pulled it shut, and locked it. "This better be good. My coffee's getting cold."

"I can make you a cup. I do have a coffeemaker." He didn't sound quite like his normal relaxed self. Slink sensed the tension, too, and began bounding around us in long strides as we moved up the street.

He opened his gate, and Slink dove through, brushing against my leg, and leaping lightly up to the front door. Alex unhooked her leash, then opened the door.

I hesitated a second, remembering the fear that had spiked through me yesterday when I'd turned and seen Harry with a gun in his hand.

The aroma of coffee and warm bread wafted through the air, and Slink trotted away into the kitchen, weaving around the laundry basket and a backpack in the hallway floor. The sound of Slink drinking from her bowl came from the kitchen. My flash of fear evaporated. It was just a normal cottage, a home, now. No desperate con men lurking around.

Alex wound the leash into a tight circle. "You're right. I do live with someone."

"A woman," I said crisply. "I saw the pink bathrobe, and the flowered mug. And the hair scrunchy in your car. Don't tell me you are fond of pink bathrobes and like mugs with daisies."

"No. Let me show you."

He went to the door beside the hallway bath, a door that had been closed when I had been in the house with Harry. He tilted it open to reveal a twin bed with a hot pink comforter and several frilly pillows, including one pillow shaped like a large initial "G." Posters of boy bands covered the daisy print wallpaper, and a tangle of clothes in every color of the rainbow was heaped on a white rocking chair.

"My sister," Alex said. "She's twelve."

I spun toward him, irritated and relieved. I punched his arm, perhaps a bit harder than I should have. "Are you serious? Your *sister*? Why didn't you tell me?"

That tiny half grin appeared again. "I should have known you wouldn't react like other girls."

"How do other girls react?"

"Either a frozen smile that doesn't reach their eyes or a gushy 'how sweet.' In either case, that's usually the last I see of them. Once they know, they're usually out of here." Alex looked down at the coiled leash as he moved it around in his hands an inch at a time. "I like you, Kate. I should have been upfront with you. I should have told you right away, but Grace is away at boarding school. She usually comes home on weekends, but this weekend she's visiting a friend's house."

"I see."

"She wasn't home last month when you were here, and to be honest, I didn't know if you were coming back, so I didn't mention it. Then you *did* come back, and I knew I should tell you." He sighed. "But I kept putting it off. Things were going so well. And then this whole thing with the fire and being a suspect...well, that made it worse. I felt I should sort that out first. I'm Grace's guardian. I couldn't let myself be carted off to prison, but you've taken care of that, exposing Hector—or Harry —whatever his name is."

"Why are you her guardian? You and...Grace...aren't orphans, are you? Didn't you say something about your dad a while back?"

"Yes. Dad's in the diplomatic service. He's in South America right now. He and my mom divorced when I was seventeen. My mom got custody of me and Grace." He scanned the room then said, "My mom felt it was quite a triumph at the time, a win over my dad. But she isn't what you'd call the motherly type."

"Hmm...I'm familiar."

"She's in Switzerland right now. I think. Last I heard, that's where she was. Grace was having some issues last year. She needed a change of scene, so I worked out the guardianship thing with my mom and moved Grace here to Nether Woodsmoor. It's turned out all right. She's settled down and seems to be doing fine now. I'm close enough that Grace can come home on the weekends."

"But it's put a cramp in your love life."

"Yeah." He put the leash down on the hall table on a lopsided stack of mail. "I'm sorry, Kate. I should have told you, but it was one of those things that the longer it went on, the harder it was to bring up."

I studied him for a moment, then said, "Do you have any other skeletons in your closet? You're not using an assumed identity and living on money scammed off innocent people? Anything like that?"

"No. Nothing so glamorous. Just one slightly emotional almost-teenager in my life."

I wasn't quite sure what I was signing up for, but I said, "Okay. I can live with that. Now, you said something about coffee?"

$\sim$

"WHY DIDN'T you mention Alex had a sister?" I asked Louise.

Louise shook her head. "That's for him to tell."

Alex and I had lingered over that cup of coffee, talking at his kitchen table until nearly noon, then decided to walk down to the pub for lunch. Alex had gone to speak to a few of the bike riders who were gathered at the bar.

Louise removed our empty plates as I said, "I just can't believe it didn't come up in passing. Not once?"

Louise shrugged. "Well, it's a given here. Grace arrives for a few days and then she's off again."

Louise propped her tray on her hip and leaned against the high table. "But now this kerfuffle about this Hector/Harry chap. Can you believe it? I want all the details."

"Yes, everyone does." The word was out that I'd been part of Harry's escape plan, which was all anyone seemed to be talking about. "But I think I'll have to tell you later," I said, spotting Quimby approaching the table as Alex returned.

Alex looked wary, but Quimby only nodded to him and turned to me.

"Ms. Sharp. Just a quick word. Can you come to the church hall today to finalize your statement?"

"Yes, of course."

"Good. Good. See DS Olney. Oh, and you'll be interested in this, I'm sure. The forensics team took apart the stone wall that Lyster helped repair. They were quite excited to find a stone slightly smaller than a man's hand with traces of blood on it. I think we have our murder weapon, Ms. Sharp, which, if we can lift any trace of Lyster's DNA from it will go a long way to insuring he serves time for the murder as well as the fraud. He was trying to be clever and hide it in plain sight. Thanks for sharing the tip with me and not tearing apart the wall on your own."

Was there a bit of reproach in his tone? If there was, I ignored it. "Well, thank you for letting me know. And Rafe?"

"He's already posted on his blog about how he was nearly taken in by a scam."

"So he's going to get away with it?"

"Oh no. The fraud concerning the letters, that's difficult to prove, but our investigation into the fire and vandalism continues. Mr. Farraday will have to answer for that and his academic career is over, I understand." Quimby looked at his watch. "Now, if you'll excuse me," he turned slightly away, then checked his movement. "After you sign your statement, you are free to leave for America at any time. Good-bye Ms. Sharp."

Alex watched until Quimby was seated at the bar before he took his seat again.

I said, "I think that was a very polite, British way of saying, go home and get out of my hair."

"You're not thinking about going back to the States, are you?" Alex asked.

"What else can I do? I have to work." I gripped his arm. "My airline ticket. I have to go." I hopped down off the barstool. "I completely forgot about it. I hope the price hasn't gone up. I put off buying it in the hope that something would work out, but I can't wait any longer. The price is already pushing the limit of my credit card as it is."

"Hold on," Alex said, "I'll walk back with you."

I was already moving through the pub, envisioning some computer algorithm kicking into effect and the prices jumping. I pushed through the pub door and ran directly into a woman in black biking shorts and a matching competition spandex shirt.

"Oh, sorry." I stepped back and held the door for her then realized as she removed her bike helmet that it was Elise DuPont.

"Just the person I wanted to see," she said. "Do you have a moment?"

"No, actually, I'm sorry. Urgent business."

"I understand you not wanting to speak to me." She took off her sunglasses, and I realized she wasn't glaring at me. "I behaved quite abominably. I'd like to apologize, if you can give me a moment."

I blinked and let the pub door fall closed behind me. I glanced at Alex, but he gave a tiny shrug.

"I'll walk with you, if you'd like," Elise said.

"Ah—sure." I gestured in the direction of Cottage Lane, and she fell into step with Alex and me.

"So, it seems I was misinformed about you, and I made certain...assumptions. It is no secret that your former boss and I did not get on. I let that prejudice me against you. It has come to my attention that you didn't cut any corners to get where you are now. On top of that, I've been informed that you are the person I should thank for exposing Rafe Farraday as a liar and a fraud."

Her little speech had stunned me so much, that I'd been speechless, but I did manage to get out a few words. "Thank me? Are you sure?"

"Yes, of course. I meant what I said earlier. I can't have my documentary be the vehicle used to perpetuate a lie and a fraud. Horrible for me and everyone involved. That would be the end of my credibility. I am sincerely grateful that you uncovered the truth."

"You're welcome." I couldn't quite believe the transformation from shrew to graciousness personified, but I wasn't going to be tacky.

"So that brings me to another point," she said. "The documentary had been structured around Rafe's revelations. Now the whole thing must be revamped. The network is still interested, thank goodness. I told them I'd like to include a section on weird and wacky claims related to Jane Austen. A sort of debunking of Austen myths. I believe it should include a recent fraud allegedly perpetrated during the filming of a recent documentary."

I looked at her closely. Was there a twinkle in her eye? If it were anyone else I would have thought she was poking fun at herself, but this was Elise. She didn't have a sense of humor.

"That's good. I'm glad for you." I shot a quick look at Alex. I was relieved for him, too. It would mean continued work for him.

"It could be good for you, too," Elise said.

Yes, there was a definite twinkle.

"If you would agree to come back to work," she added.

I stopped walking and turned toward her.

"Several of the scenes we filmed were based on Rafe's information. Pure fiction, as it turns out. I will spend this afternoon rehashing the budget and working on a new script, which will involve new scenes, which will require more location scouting.

Alex assures me that he cannot manage our current location shoots as well as look for new ones on his own, and I agree with him. We need another location scout. Can I convince you to return to the production?"

I was slightly suspicious of this new and improved Elise, but a job was a job. And I'd get to stay in Nether Woodsmoor, at least for a while. "Yes, I'm very interested. I'm sure we can work something out."

"Brilliant. Welcome back." Elise held out her hand, and I shook it. She gave me a quick nod and turned back to the inn, then called over her shoulder, "Five-thirty a.m. tomorrow. Don't be late."

"So the old Elise isn't entirely gone," I said as I watched her go.

"I told you she wasn't a complete ogre."

"She did apologize very nicely. So few people actually apologize these days. Usually they just give a long list of excuses and 'say sorry if I offended you,' which isn't an apology at all." I turned to give Alex my whole attention. "Did you have anything to do with that?"

"No. The word was out about Rafe yesterday. I told her we needed you back on board, but I've been telling her that since she fired you."

"Hmm. Well, we'll see how long she stays like this. Did you have a feeling she was the Wicked Witch of the West doing her best to imitate Glinda, the Good Witch?"

"No, I didn't think that," Alex said with a laugh. "But now that you mention it…"

I looked after her disappearing back. "I should have asked for a car before agreeing, shouldn't I? Now we're both without wheels. You'll have to join me, hoofing it across the fields to our shooting locations."

"I'm sure we'll manage."

"Right. So, I'm staying," I said, looking at him, happiness bubbling up inside me.

"Excellent. I'm glad." He extended his hand.

"Me, too," I said, linking my fingers through his. "Now, I believe you promised to show me a castle ruin today."

THE END

～

Stay up to date with with Sara. Sign up for her updates and get exclusive content and giveaways.

～

RETURN TO NETHER Woodsmoor and join Kate when she becomes involved in a locked room mystery at Parkview Hall in Death in a Stately Home, available in ebook, audio, and print.

Good houseguests don't get accused of murder . . .

KATE SHARP LOVES the perks of her location scout profession. When she fills in for a researcher at a Regency-themed English house party, she's looking forward to indulging in the posh atmosphere of tea on the lawn and elegant candlelight dinners, but when the guest next-door is murdered in a locked room, Kate becomes the prime suspect.

As she turns her attention to the guests, the staff, and the owners, Kate must unlock the mystery and uncover the murderer before she's arrested for a crime she didn't commit.

Death in a Stately Home is the third installment in the Murder on Location collection, a series of British cozy mysteries. If you love engaging characters, compelling British detective mysteries, the works of Jane Austen, and vivid locations that transport you to another place, then you'll love *USA Today* bestselling author Sara Rosett's latest whodunit.

THE STORY BEHIND THE STORY

Thank you for reading *Death in an English Cottage*. I had so much fun returning to Nether Woodsmoor for this second book in the *Murder on Location* series.

Kate and Alex will return in another adventure. If you'd like me to drop you a line when I have a new book coming out, sign up for my newsletter at SaraRosett.com/signup/2. You'll also get exclusive early looks at upcoming books as well as member-only giveaways.

If you enjoyed *Death in an English Cottage*, I'd appreciate it if you posted an online review. Even something as short as a few lines can help potential readers figure out whether or not the book is their cup of tea. Thanks!

If you'd like more England and Derbyshire in particular, check out my Death in the English Countryside pinboard on Pinterest to see places I visited on my research trip as well as articles and specific locales that inspired me.

ABOUT THE AUTHOR

USA Today bestselling author Sara Rosett writes fun mysteries. Her books are light-hearted escapes for readers who enjoy interesting settings, quirky characters, and puzzling mysteries. *Publishers Weekly* called Sara's books, "satisfying," "well-executed," and "sparkling."

Sara loves to get new stamps in her passport and considers dark chocolate a daily requirement. Find out more at SaraRosett.com.

Connect with Sara
www.SaraRosett.com

CPSIA information can be obtained
at www.ICGtesting.com
Printed in the USA
LVHW092149170723
752733LV00038B/605